A SAGE'S SANCTUARY PREQUEL

THE QUIET SIDE

 CASEY BLAIR

THE QUIET SIDE
A Sage's Sanctuary Prequel

Copyright © 2025 Casey Blair,
All rights reserved.

No part of this edition may be reproduced, distributed, transmitted, or used in any manner whatsoever without permission in writing from the author, except in the case of brief quotations in a book review. For permission requests, email Casey@CaseyBlair.com.

No AI Training: Without in any way limiting the author's exclusive rights under copyright, any use of this publication to "train" generative artificial intelligence (AI) technologies is expressly prohibited.

This book is a work of fiction. No AI tools were used in its creation. Names, characters, places, and events are either the product of the author's imagination or are used fictitiously. Any resemblance to actual persons, living or dead, events, or locales is entirely coincidental.

Cover design by Miblart, 2025.
Dragon frame by Alderdoodle, 2025.
Hardcase cover art by Kateryna Vitkovska, 2025.
Developmental editing by Zola Hartley, 2025.
Copyediting and proofreading by Adie Hart, 2025.
Author photograph by Mariah Bush, 2013.

Ebook ISBN: 9798998829505
Paperback ISBN: 9798998829512
Hardcover ISBN: 9798998829529

www.caseyblair.com

For Claire.

May all our hearts leave such an impression on the world, lasting beyond us in everyone whose lives we touch.

CONTENTS

Chapter 1	1
Chapter 2	19
Chapter 3	40
Chapter 4	52
Chapter 5	71
Chapter 6	89
Chapter 7	98
Chapter 8	116
Chapter 9	136
Epilogue	153
Thank You	160
About the Author	161
Also By	162

CHAPTER 1

KOVAN

Sanctuary Isle has only one entrance, and it's blocked to me.

Not because the tide is up, covering the land that attaches the island to the rest of the empire.

Because I am weak.

Even this far out from the temple where just weeks ago the Sage of Wrath created the magical dampening field that now prevents magic from being worked inside, I can feel its strength eclipsing my own.

Whispers have started calling it the Quiet.

Only Learned Muka, first among my mentors—*my handlers*, whispers my traitorous mind—is here to watch me fail as the water rises at my feet where I stand on the Precipice, the line where the Quiet extends to.

I'm one man facing the biggest magical working I've ever felt, which normally would energize me.

Not today.

Learned Muka supported my request to send away the audience, to allow me space to meditate on the huge task before me.

But leaving me alone on a magical and existential precipice, both physically and with my thoughts, is not helping. Quite the opposite.

The priesthood wants the dampening field down. The military arm of priests who were deployed with the sage on Sanctuary Isle must all be dead, but no one can confirm that or offer them burial rites, because no government officials can reach any villagers who still live at Crystal Hollow, the town at the foot of the mountain where Celestial Sanctuary Temple sits.

I am powerful enough to cross the Precipice, at the very least, even if it would leave me powerless on the other side.

The Quiet side.

But am I powerful enough to tear down Wrath's final work?

Possibly. Other sages have tried and failed, which is why I, the strongest remaining sage of our generation, have been taken from my duties to make the attempt.

The problem is that as the Sage of Resolve, my strength depends on my determination.

And for once, I have mixed feelings about the task assigned to me.

Not just because I have always thought of my power as one of augmentation: strengthening roots to support greater growth.

But because the priests fear the talk that the Sage of Wrath's repudiation is a sign the gods have turned away from them. That without the unified front of the living avatars of the gods, and Wrath especially, the empire's threat is weakened. They want her, and all the sages, under tighter control than ever.

At first, I resented what her action had cost the rest of us.

Now, I wonder if she revealed a truth that I have been willfully denying for years.

That my resolve has enabled me in the doing.

Quiet steps behind me; damning.

Learned Muka has long since learned that sound will not crack my resolve—this is another sign of the priesthood's desperation.

"Sage Kovan," she chastises. "You will not firm your strength by holding still."

Which is exactly why I am not moving through one of my katas, the movement patterns sages use to build and flow our divine power through to the world.

I fear I will not find my resolve at all. That I do not have the strength of *character* to match Wrath.

Or, more egregious: I will find it, and my resolve will make everything worse.

I could pretend to fail, but I have never given up in my life—I would have to spend the rest of my days choosing inaction over and over.

Maybe that will buy me time, to have the balls to make a real choice. About something that matters, that no one else *can* choose. Choices that would never have occurred to me without the Sage of Wrath's coup.

Maybe, maybe—

My senses ping first, a growing, enormous magical presence closing in rapidly from ahead of me—

—Magic coming *from* the Quiet.

My first thought is that it's Wrath—shameful relief as I think she has come to own responsibility for the choice, taking it back out of my hands—but a second later I realize the feel of the magic is different.

A dragon.

A different kind of relief, combined with adrenaline.

"Dragon incoming from Sanctuary," I snap to Learned Muka. "I'll hold."

Because holding, at least, I can do.

Forever, if I have to.

A sharp intake of breath, but Learned Muka has decades of training on me and is retreating an instant later to gather my escort and call for reinforcements.

Priests can only fight dragons by combining their power, chanting spells in unison.

But a sage—

A single sage might hold off a dragon.

As a figure emerges from the mist, though, my doubts flourish anew.

Because this is surely a dragon. The immortal grace, the shock of blue hair, the sheer menace radiating from such a slim form—they're all giveaways, even if I didn't have my magic.

But I *can* clearly sense the dragon's magic, even on the Quiet side of the Precipice where they remain—which means dragon magic may still work there, while human magic will not.

(An oversight from the Sage of Wrath, or a failure—or an intended consequence?)

Most damningly: dragons do not approach priests in human form unless they have a death wish.

Maybe I'm not the only one shaken by Wrath's choice.

On instinct, my body flows through a quick pattern, falling into a stance as I swirl my arms in a deliberate form to back up my voice, the lie of feeling strength surging through me as I thrust a hand forward and intone, "*Stop.*"

My power emerges from my hand like a pale flash of light, bathing the dragon in a field of shimmering gold.

A very wispy gold, from me. My magic crosses the Precipice, but even at this far edge of the Quiet, it's muted.

But, wonder of wonders, the dragon does stop.

It's a bad sign that I'm surprised by my own effectiveness.

That I wonder if he in fact stops because he is *humoring* me, not because my resolve is powerful enough to meet him in this situation.

"A sage alone," the man—the dragon—says in a low, threatening voice. "I'd begun to wonder if that ever happened."

Familiar resolve pools in my gut, like reassurance, like nausea. The priests aren't wrong about everything—this man has been hunting us; the dragons *are* our enemies.

Unfortunately, that doesn't mean they are right about everything.

"The priests will return soon, but I am as close to alone now as I am permitted to be," I tell him, a challenge in my voice. "Do your worst."

It is weak to depend on an external challenge to find my own resolve, but right now a fight is just what I need to feel grounded again. To feel like the ground is solid beneath my feet instead of ever-changing waves—

But the dragon lets out a sound of disgust. "Permitted?" he echoes incredulously.

And that's all.

Is he—waiting on clarification?

Am I about to have a *conversation* with a dragon, rather than a battle?

My feet are definitely submerged in water.

I continue moving through a form, but it's a ponderous, holding one; a gathering, so I will be ready when it is time to act.

Ha.

"No one person should have so much power without oversight," I say slowly. "Before the priests took on that role, a sage killed an emperor."

The dragon snorts, smoke coming out of his nose even in human form.

That probably means his dragon form is very close to the surface, and I'll need to defend against his fire.

I subtly shift my movements with that goal in mind.

"Perhaps the emperor needed to be killed, did you ever wonder about that?" the dragon snaps. "Perhaps some priests need to be too, though that's hardly news." And before I can reply, he adds, "And now a sage has refused to kill on command. Tell me, do you think your choices are more fallible than hers, or less?"

It hits me all at once that what I'm hearing from this dragon is *anger*.

Toward... me? The priesthood, humans? The way the world is? I can't tell.

"It's not my job to choose," I tell him, even as my heart twists, because choosing what to grow is outside my remit; because no wonder I'm having so much trouble today, with the prospect of making a choice of my own, the realization that perhaps I never have, have only defaulted to what others chose for me; and that in itself may be a choice, but it may also simply be an abnegation, and *that* is counter to what I am supposed to stand for. "It's my job to be a divine vessel."

"Oh, I see." His voice is bitter; his movements jerky. *Any moment now.* "So that's how they do it? They convince you that nothing you do with your power is your responsibility, because you're not the one who chooses, and you shouldn't be the one. Then why do you individually embody the spirit of the gods, I wonder?"

I am having a conversation with a dragon.

A dragon who, despite my wariness, *my* desperation, has made no move toward actually attacking me. Infuriating, and probably lulling me into a false sense of security so that I will let down my guard, but—

The priests still aren't here.

"Do you know why the Sage of Wrath created the dampening field?"

The question slips out before I realize I even want to know, let alone that I'm going to ask.

The dragon looks back at me with scorn.

"If you can't guess," the dragon says, "you are irredeemably stupid. And I'm not here to provide you with justifications that you'll let the priests twist into whatever serves their narrative."

I stop breathing for a moment.

Maybe we are in a battle after all.

I am resolve incarnate.

I will *not* stop moving just because a dragon's words hit me like a barrel to the chest.

But my movements slow to the speed of molasses, because I cannot for the life of me decide how to respond.

And in that moment, I know that no matter how our confrontation ends, the dragon has already won.

He's right, and he's wrong. I don't want justifications for the priests.

I want justifications for *me*.

I want to know whether she was right, so that I know if I'm right.

Right here, right now, I can make the biggest statement any sage ever has. I can unwork what the Sage of Wrath may have given her life to accomplish, and in so doing change the nature of understanding of sages and divinity.

Or I can hold still.

And it galls me that I am not sure I have the resolve to do either.

That I am not as strong as I, or anyone else, thought.

That the Sage of Wrath could do so much, and that I, ostensibly her equal, cannot do anything.

That perhaps not only am I insignificant now, but—counter to what I've believed—I always have been, and can only *be* insignificant, because of who I am.

I hear commotion behind us, and instead of relief—that the priests are here, that they will take this choice out of my hands—all I feel is dismay. The chance for me to do *anything* that matters is slipping away.

I stare at the dragon, who is beginning to back away into the fog leading to the island as the gold light fades and the resolve of my command holding him falters—or he wants me to believe that was what was holding him—and stop moving entirely.

The gold of my power vanishes.

And yet the dragon freezes now in truth.

"I'm here to take down the dampening field," I tell him.

Shouts behind me; the priests can see that I've stopped moving and will think something is wrong.

And indeed something is.

"*I* am not irredeemably stupid," the dragon snarls back. "Congratulations, your cowardice will recreate tenfold the conditions that pushed the Sage of Wrath to this."

That is what I am afraid of.

That having finally realized I alone can make a difference, I will make exactly the wrong kind. That I will drown a seed rather than nurture it.

That maybe I have the *worst* kind of significance: the kind that supports the wrong side.

A strange realization settles on me; almost disbelieving.

"I can't do it," I say, more to myself. "I don't have the resolve." But then I meet the dragon's icy eyes head-on as I add, "I don't think I have the resolve to fight you, either. If you go now, you can escape unscathed. They won't follow you to Sanctuary now, not with the tide coming up and no idea what to expect on the other side."

I still don't know what he hoped to gain here. If for some reason it was to keep the dampening field up, he has it.

But though he may have been hunting sages before, he didn't attack me here.

If a dragon can make that choice, so can a sage.

"Maybe not irredeemable," the dragon mutters, or at least I think he does—an instant later he is in his dragon form, sparkling like moonstone and the size of a house, and this close to him I can *feel* the heat shimmering off his scales as he takes a menacing step toward me.

Toward the Precipice.

Gods, maybe I am irredeemably stupid after all.

Then the dragon's voice sounds in my mind.

«I can take you somewhere the priests won't be able to get to you, if you want the chance to make your own choices,» he says. «But decide fast.»

Because the priests are here, their chants screaming as they close in behind us, and we only have seconds before they will be throwing every spell they have at this dragon whose only known sin has been existing—and perhaps undermining my faith; their power over me.

But even that blame I can't lay at the dragon's feet.

I have no idea where the dragon means to take me. He could bring me to a dragon's den. He could abandon me on a mountaintop. He hasn't injured me physically, but that's a far cry from enough reason for me to actively trust him.

It doesn't matter.

He's offering a chance; a light of direction in an otherwise flailing abyss.

And more than that, he's offering me *time*.

The barest hint of resolve flares in me, and I seize it.

"Please," I whisper.

Somehow the dragon hears it.

The powerful burst of his wings doesn't blow me back only because I have used my magic to anchor myself against his wind, a gold glow—stronger now—in the early morning light.

My stomach drops at the realization that he's leaving me after all, to the same situation—

THE QUIET SIDE

And then a shadow falls over me, *past* the Precipice, instants before claws close around my torso and pull me into the air.

The priests fire their spells, blasts of colorful magic that must hit on this side, because the dragon roars—in anger perhaps; or pain.

But he doesn't drop me.

Another powerful beat of his wings, and we are—*I* am—on the Quiet side.

Out of the priests' reach.

For now.

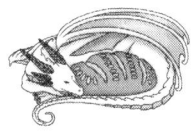

THE DRAGON IS HOLDING me so tightly I can't breathe, the autumn trees below a blur of color overwhelming my vision. I scramble to perform a kata only to feel my power vanish in a rush, like the life has been drained out of me.

The sensation, along with the lack of air, accomplish what nothing else ever has, even in the worst of my sage training.

I black out.

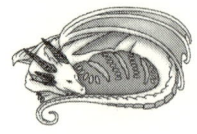

I WAKE TO THE feeling of being shoved.

My training takes over, and I roll to my feet into the stance for a kata—

—only to feel *no power* thrumming through me.

I freeze—like a weakling, like *prey*—

«Finally,» the dragon's voice snorts in my head.

I jolt again, turning to see him standing behind me, bone-white scales glinting in the morning sunlight.

I can barely even sense a dragon.

There's only one place that means I can be, and sure enough, behind the dragon looms Celestial Sanctuary Temple... on the mountain of Sanctuary Isle.

We're in the Quiet.

Where the Sage of Wrath detonated a working so massive, magic no longer functions inside.

Except, evidently, dragon magic.

I'm in danger.

Yet somehow, I don't feel like it.

The dragon could kill me, easily. I could do nothing to resist his magical flame. He could *step* on me—that must have been the shove I felt.

But death isn't the worst fate for me. That, he's already saved me from.

Shame coils in my gut at the thought, and I lash out.

"Your kidnapping skills need some work," I snap. "Humans need to breathe."

"I don't make a habit of kidnapping humans," the dragon snaps back.

That startles me into a frown.

Of course dragons kidnap humans. They need humans to mate, and dragons take any offspring with them back to wherever dragons live. What a bizarre thing to protest—

—Unless this specific dragon doesn't?

"What are you doing here, then?"

I am completely unprepared for the dragon to look away from me. Almost as if he's... embarrassed?

To be caught among humans and *not* be preying on them?

«The Sage of Wrath is still inside the temple,» the dragon says, and I'm not sure if that's an answer to my question or changing the subject.

Either way, it surprises me. To have created a working this powerful, I had thought she'd have needed to give up her life. "How do you know?"

The dragon glares at me. «You're a sage. Can you get inside?»

"You can't?"

The dragon lets out a snort of fire. My eyes widen and my heart rate kicks up, even though it wasn't directed at me.

There is something going on here I don't understand, and I don't think asking the dragon questions is going to get me answers that don't burn me, one way or another.

I walk around the dragon to approach the temple. He stomps around me, as if fighting his own instincts to allow me to, despite the fact that he asked me to try this.

But the closer I get to the door, it's like the air around me thickens, like I am trying to walk through a swamp that slows me further with every step.

I grit my teeth and strain, my muscles protesting more every second but I am *resolve* gods curse it—

Then it's like the air itself turns solid and *shoves* against me.

I fly backwards, and only years of training have me flipping to land on my feet.

I gape at the temple.

«You were supposed to use magic,» the dragon growls at me.

"I don't have any here," I say absently, still stunned. Did he think it would be different because I'm a sage? Is this one place immune to dragon magic? "You're sure Yora's still in there? Alive?"

The dragon goes still. «Her name is Yora.»

"The Sage of Wrath, yes." Did he... not know that? Then—

I frown toward the temple. "Where are all the priests? They wouldn't have all been inside."

«Dead.»

"But then—"

«I burned them to ash,» the dragon snaps.

I stare at the dragon, reeling. Had they all been dead then, truly, or did the dragon kill them?

Does it matter? Is it better if it was the dragon responsible for their deaths, rather than a sage? I mentally shy away from the question, though some part of myself deep within believes I will need to answer that question for myself.

"Then there are no burial rites to administer," I mutter absently. That was one of the goals for the priests in getting the dampening field down.

«Better than... the Sage of Wrath waking up surrounded by rotting corpses.»

"Wake up?"

The dragon glares at me, as if daring me to disagree.

He needn't bother. I literally have no resolve in me right now. What would I even argue?

«I have to go,» the dragon says abruptly.

Then again, maybe I can argue after all. "*Go?*" I echo. "You're just going to leave me here? Alone on a mountain?"

«Better than surrounded on a mountain,» the dragon says irritably. «I told you the priests wouldn't be able to track you, not that you would have servants to attend your every whim.»

"That's not—"

«Unless you want to come freeze with me at the top of the mountain while I hibernate?» he interrupts coolly.

Of course. Dragons changing form takes a lot of energy—it's why the priests always want to force them into situations where they transform, or find them sleeping, because when they take their dragon forms they have a limited time before they *have* to sleep. And that's when they're vulnerable.

Which means the dragon took an extra risk for me.

Is taking an even bigger one now, in fact, by telling me where he's going. Although he could be lying—if he flies high enough, he'll be out of range of my magical senses.

On the heels of that thought I notice that some of his scales are more slate, charred, than white. "Will you be able to manage?" I ask gruffly, staring at them.

The dragon flexes his scales somehow, and a cascade flows off of him onto the ground. The scales revealed beneath are still darker, more pale smoke than pearl, but they definitely look healthier.

An unexpected relief, to be glad I didn't get a dragon hurt.

Though now of course it occurs to me that after exposing himself to me, he may wish for me to believe he is not such easy prey as that.

He doesn't trust me any more than I trust him—less, probably.

Guilt churns inside my gut that I absolutely don't *deserve* the trust of a being who just did me an enormous boon.

«Yes,» the dragon says curtly, cutting through my spiraling thoughts. «Good luck.»

Oh, shit. "Wait, what I am I supposed to—"

With a powerful flap of his wings that blows wind and dirt into my face before I can block it, the dragon takes off.

"—do," I finish uselessly.

I'd thought the prospect of a dragon abandoning me on a mountain was catastrophizing, but here I am.

But as if he still heard me, the dragon's voice growls one last time in my head, fainter with every word as he rapidly ascends into the sky, «Figure it out yourself, for once in your life.»

Anger burgeons in me, chasing his words.

That may have been the best parting gift he could have given me.

Because I *am* angry—with him, and with the priests, and with Yora, and with myself—and that is so much better than flailing.

I don't know what I'm doing.

I don't have magic to help me, or guidance.

Only myself.

And if I depend on anything else for my determination, it's no wonder I can't enter the Sage of Wrath's temple.

So: take stock.

I need food and shelter.

Ironic, that now I am suddenly free to plant whatever seed I wish to grow but have no notion of how to do so.

In the early morning, I hear birds chirping, but without my magic I have no skills to catch them. I feel the sun on my face, stronger than where I was before; a sign of just how high up I am. And the gentle breeze is an ominous portent of the chill to come when the sun goes down.

This high up, the mountain will get bitterly cold by the time night falls, and without the magic of my determination, no amount of resolve will prevent me from getting frostbite.

I can't access the temple and whatever food stores are there, not that I know how to cook them anyway.

I can't descend the mountain, because the magic dampening field is thinner there—the priests might be able to find me, and I'm not ready for that yet. My resolve didn't falter through starvation training, though it's true that I knew then that food still *existed*. I knew the training would have an end, if not when.

Maybe I will have to resolve to believe that now, too—that this situation, that my failures that created it—will have an end. Even if I'm not yet sure how.

I turn around, surveying the temple grounds.

Only then do I notice that there's a cottage.

There has never been a cottage here on my previous visits to the temple. The priests who maintain the temple and any visitors have always been housed inside.

Is it new? That would mean someone has been up here since the Sage of Wrath's working—her Quieting.

The dragon? Despite how he challenged my expectations today, I find I can't quite imagine him there.

Probably it's not occupied, simply some part of temple administration that sages are never troubled with.

But: there may still be food, or at least warmth.

A possibility.

I take my first step, and begin walking toward it.

CHAPTER 2

TASA

The hike back up the mountain is... brisk. The mountain air is fresh! The sun is shining! It's a good day.

It *is* a good day.

I shouldn't need to tell myself that so forcefully.

Even though the reason I am up this early is to work on salvage before the villagers who've known me their whole life open their doors to glare at me, and the reason I'm returning to my new home on the mountain now is to avoid the oppressive weight of judgment when I inevitably get in their way.

I shouldn't complain. After the magical shockwave a few weeks ago, I'm better off than many of them, and the aftermath gave me a job that no one else can do. *And* now I have a home all to myself where none of them can get to me. I can just be *me*.

The trees open up as I reach the clearing where Celestial Sanctuary Temple and now also my cottage sit. It looks almost... shimmery? in the early morning light today, filling me with both wonder and a kind of twisted longing.

Just because I nullify magic by existing doesn't mean I don't crave it in my heart.

As I make my way to the door, though, I finally see what the glimmers catching my eye actually are: dragon scales.

They're *everywhere*.

And some of them are very, very dark.

Was there a dragon fight in my front yard while I was at the base of the mountain? Surely I would have noticed that, right?

My heart clenches. No. There's a long list of things I ought to have noticed.

But my cottage is still standing, and the ground doesn't look super singed?

But those dark scales...

I hurry to my door, letting my pack full of materials for my cottage—I've never built a planter, but how hard can it be? Yes, I know, famous last words—drop unceremoniously to the ground in my rush.

But just as I'm about to reach the door, it opens.

On a person. A stranger.

Inside my house.

We stare at each other.

He's... incredibly attractive, in an extremely intimidating way, not helped by his all-black ensemble. Tall, with dark hair, practically golden eyes, sharp cheekbones, severe expression. Like he doesn't know how to smile.

My heart rate kicks up. Meticulous people with high expectations who aren't forgiving of mistakes are... not the kind of people I do well with.

Is he a priest? He must be, with this outfit, right? But no priests have been here since the blast. Though I guess technically I don't own this land, but I really didn't think that would be a problem all things considered—

"Who are you?" the man asks abruptly.

"Tasa," I answer automatically, before realizing maybe I shouldn't have.

I sigh. That's me. Always speaking before thinking.

Too late now.

I guess having a space of my own was too good to be true for me. "You're here to evict me," I gather, resigned.

His eyebrows shoot up. "This cottage is yours?"

What's that supposed to mean?

I square my shoulders. "Yes. I built it. I'm sorry, I know I didn't have permission, but because of the magic I didn't think anyone else would be back here—"

"You built it *since* the Sage of Wrath's working?"

I blink. "...Yes?"

He's frowning now. "That was only weeks ago."

I'm beginning to feel like we're having two different conversations.

"Yes," I say slowly. "The shockwave wiped out a lot of the magic that was embedded in the Crystal Hollow's infrastructure. I've been sorting through and salvaging what I could. So a lot of these pieces were still functional; I just had to combine them."

Which is why, yes, my cottage looks a little... sloping. Okay fine, lopsided, and mismatched besides. It's a weird amalgamation of a bunch of different houses and stores and whatever else.

But *I* made it what it is. It's *mine*.

Or I thought it was, a few minutes ago.

The man's eyebrows draw down. "That's incredibly dangerous," he tells me. "Destabilized magical workings—"

"I'm a null," I explain.

His jaw snaps shut as he stares some more.

How did he think I was managing to live here at the epicenter?

Come to think of it, how is *he* functioning here? It's pretty uncomfortable for anyone with a little magic, and dire for anyone with more—so, you know, that covers literally everyone but me—to be here.

"So you're... not here to evict me," I say slowly.

He blinks. "What? No."

I officially have no idea what's going on.

"But you let yourself into my house," I point out.

"I didn't know anyone lived here."

Is... *he* defensive now?

"But now you do, and you're blocking the doorway so I can't come in?"

That visibly startles him. He mutters something under his breath and runs a hand through his hair, mussing it further.

I missed that, before; his hair is mussed, like the wind has blown it every which way.

Actually it looks like it might have some leaves in it.

Maybe he's not quite as uptight as he appears.

And an extremely attractive uptight stranger looking mussed in my house should definitely not look so appealing.

"My apologies," he says stiffly, stepping back. "Please, come in."

And then he winces—I'm guessing at the realization that he just invited me into my own house.

"Thank you," I say easily, smoothing over the moment—distracting people from mistakes, my specialty born of necessity—and cross the threshold.

Into my house, where a mysterious handsome stranger has intruded.

"Don't you need your things?" he asks gruffly.

"Oh!" In the shock of seeing him here, I'd forgotten why I was in such a rush to get inside. "Is everything okay? I saw the dragon scales out front and wasn't sure if—ah, someone had been hurt?"

There I go again, belatedly realizing that telling a priest I'm worried about a dragon is maybe not my best move.

My attempt to cover was in vain, because Intense Man zeroes in on me immediately. "Do you recognize the scales?"

Ah! Easy sidestep. "No. But I saw a lot of charcoal ones, and I thought maybe they were scorched. People tend to be hurt if there have been fires around."

"Have there been fires here?" he asks.

Uh. You could say that.

"Is that why you're here?" I ask in a determinedly light tone. "Do the priests think a dragon is responsible for what happened? Because I can tell you there weren't any scales when I first came up after the shockwave."

The priest looks startled again, like I've bopped him on the nose. Surprisingly endearing.

But then alarm fills me as he visibly deflates.

Worried he's about to fall over, I rush over to support him and walk him backwards to the nearest chair, which he drops into with a profoundly shocked expression.

Oh shit I just nullified a priest. It's not permanent on people, but still—

"Oh gods, I'm so sorry, I shouldn't have touched you without permission—"

"It's fine," he cuts me off.

I freeze.

That in no way sounds fine.

And I know better. I do. Especially now, when magic is a limited resource—

"I'm sorry," I say again, and this time my voice is a whisper.

I hate that I'm like this, that I can't seem to help it.

The man frowns up at me. "I said it's fine. I don't say things I don't mean."

Now it's my turn to blink.

"I can see that you believe that," I say slowly, "but that does... not match my experience of people. If you'll forgive me the observation, Learned."

"I'm not a priest," he says. "I'm a sage."

...Excuse me.

Excuse me, *what?!*

Oh gods. The golden eyes. They're *actual* gold, it wasn't just a trick of the light—

That's how a person who isn't a null can be here—he's not just a priest, he's *worse*—

"I apologize for intruding on your home," the sage—the *sage!!*—says, "and I have a deeply unfair favor to ask of you."

Oh no. He wants to take my cottage after all.

Where will I go now?

I mean, yes, I can build another cottage in Crystal Hollow, but the thought of living under the weight of that judgment again after my few weeks of freedom—of seeing their reaction to the build I am so proud of—makes me want to shrivel up and cry.

And then as if from a long distance, I hear the sage say stiffly, "I would like to ask if I might stay with you here for a time."

I stare at him.

He stares back at me.

I poke myself experimentally, but yep, this appears to be real life. Somehow.

Where a *sage* just *asked* if he could *move in* with *me*.

This is fine! Definitely fine.

It takes a second for the words to penetrate through my spiraling thoughts, and then some more seconds as I decide that not only did they for real just happen but also that I will have to actually respond and not just keep gaping at him like a simpleton.

I close my eyes and take a deep breath. When I open them, I look at him again.

There is a man—and, not to put too fine a point on it, an attractive man who *wants* to live with *me*, still very much not over that part—sitting in my chair who is on a mountain, alone, pale like he's had a tremendous shock, who looks like he is about to keel over off of my chair and is sitting upright solely through force of will.

Nothing in my life has prepared me to process this situation.

I drop to my butt on the floor in front of him. "I think we should start over," I say. "My name is Tasa. What's yours?"

A beat, and then he slides onto the floor in front of me and meets my eyes. "Kovan."

"Just Kovan?" I query. "Not Sage Kovan?"

"'Sage' is not my name," he says. "It is a title. And on this mountain, at this time, it is a useless one. Just Kovan."

Oookay. "Just Kovan then. It's thoughtful of you to bring yourself down to my level, but you can keep sitting in the chair. I don't mind."

"I do mind, Cottagebuilder Tasa," Kovan rumbles. "There is nothing lowering about meeting you on more even ground."

Well, that's sweet. Also, was that a hint of humor? "And there is nothing useless about being a sage here," I say. "No one else besides me has managed to get this close to the temple besides me and—" *Dammit.*

"And the dragon," the sage says dryly. "He's the one who brought me here. That must be why he thought I'd be able to get into the temple."

Oh thank goodness. "You know Zan? Is he okay?"

A pause. "Yes. He took some damage helping me escape, but he appeared to believe it wasn't serious. He will be hibernating now, however."

"Helping you *escape*? Wait—*did* you get into the temple?"

The sage's jaw clenches. "I did not."

"Damn," I mutter. And then bite my tongue. "Sorry!"

Kovan waves this off. "What did it look like when you got here?"

"Oh, gods, it was awful. There were dead bodies just... everywhere. Like they'd just dropped where they stood and ceased to breathe. And some, um. Viscera? I guess from the pressure of the shockwave? And I don't know if you've ever tried to move a dead body, but even without, uh, fluids, they are *heavy*, and handling them—" I shudder. "I was trying, but it would have been so much worse if Zan hadn't shown up."

"To help?" The sage is skeptical.

"I mean, I don't think that was his original intention, but he *did* help."

"Do you know what his original intention was?"

I narrow my eyes. We started over, but somehow I've let him interrogate me again. "Does it matter?"

The sage lets out a breath. "No. I suppose not. I am not sure if I am relieved to know that a dragon isn't responsible for killing them."

Ah.

Slower than I probably should be, but in my defense it's hard to overstate how incredibly unlikely all of this is, I'm beginning to put some pieces together here, and they're adding up to a crisis of faith.

In a *sage*. An avatar of the gods.

Immediately after *another* sage has just dramatically killed a whole bunch of priests, so this is...

Yikes.

...Well, I guess that does make more sense than a person who actually knows what they want intentionally trying to live with me.

"I know we're supposed to hate dragons," I say carefully, "but Zan seemed genuinely distressed that even I couldn't get into the temple. And when I explained how terrible it would be for a person to wake up surrounded by corpses, he didn't hesitate to help. I only know the one dragon, and it's not like we're best friends, but I don't think they are all lacking in empathy."

Kovan's golden gaze fixes on me. "It was your idea to burn them."

I lift my chin. "Yes. No one else would have been able to come for them anyway. Is that why you're here?"

The sage looks away. "More or less," he mutters.

And that's it.

"I could use a little more detail," I prompt a little hesitantly. "Like, your personal stuff is obviously your business, but while you're here, should I be expecting dragon battles? Are you going to be performing more magic that will backlash and destroy my cottage like Crystal Hollow has been destroyed?"

"Crystal Hollow has been destroyed?"

I open my mouth to answer and then and cross my arms. "You keep turning questions back on me. Is that a sage trick?"

Kovan grimaces.

Would you look at that, a powerful man who doesn't explode when you point out his flaws—more than once, even.

"In a manner of speaking," he says. "Specifically it's an interrogation tactic. My apologies. I am... unused to being in this position. But I think in this case my personal business may in fact also be your business. You deserve to know who you would be allowing into your home."

That sounds properly ominous, but I am immediately and absolutely certain he's way harder on himself than I will ever be.

Kovan squares his shoulders. "I was brought here to take down the magic dampening field. I... couldn't do it. And rather than admitting that, I allowed a dragon to spirit me away so that I did not have to face the consequences of a decision. I could have helped your village, and I did not."

A strange understanding passes through me.

I may know a thing or two about presenting yourself in absolutely the worst light.

If you do it yourself, after all, then you can't be surprised when someone hates you.

"Why couldn't you do it?" I ask.

Kovan's jaw clenches so hard that, as close as I am to him, I actually *hear* his teeth grind.

"Ah," I say.

He glares up at me. "What does that mean?"

I raise my eyebrows. "It means you chose to let your natural enemy carry you away from the system that has always insulated you, which I take to mean that your faith in said system has faltered, to say the least."

"That doesn't bother you?"

He's doing it again, but I let him. "I'm not sure if this will come as a surprise to you, but priests are not actually bearers of unconditional generosity. I may believe in divine power, but how priests exercise power in our world is a lot more suspect."

Kovan winces. "I... appreciate your honesty."

I snort. "No need to lie. No one else does."

His gaze whips back to me. "I already told you, I don't say things I don't mean."

So he did.

Oddly, I think maybe I can believe him.

A kernel of unreasonable warmth in my chest. He appreciates me. Okay, maybe not everything about me, but *something*. That's pretty good, right?

Welp, there go the warm feelings. Good job, brain.

I shift on the ground, and he tracks the motion.

I sigh internally. Great, now he's going to think I'm uncomfortable. Some host.

Then again, he did essentially break into my house. Strange that doesn't make me feel less like putting him at ease here.

Probably, it's because I very much sympathize with wanting to run away.

I just never thought my haven could be anyone else's.

Or that it might not be mine at all.

"So you want to stay with me to hide from the priesthood?" I ask matter-of-factly, as if this is a totally normal request and not utterly insane to even be entertaining.

"Yes," Kovan says slowly. "Or rather: I need to stay on this mountaintop so that they can't track me while I"—he winces—"figure out a longer-term plan."

Oh, there's a mood.

The sage continues, "I would like to stay with *you* to learn how to actually live on my own."

"What does that mean, exactly?"

"It means I don't know how to cook food, let alone acquire it," he says bluntly, then waves at the extremely uneven ceiling above us. "Or create shelter."

Oh, wow. That would be quite the learning curve.

I knew sages didn't live like the rest of us, but I'd never really thought about what that means. But if they're *that* dependent on priests—I mean, yes, it means all their needs are taken care of, but there are rumors about why the Sage of Wrath did what she did and I'm giving them more credit now.

I can't help with a crisis of faith, but survival skills—oddly, I probably *can* teach that.

I've tried pretty much every job there is, after all.

What a world, where I—and my copious collection of failures—could help a sage.

Of course, there's the small problem where he would have to live with me, because he needs to stay on this mountain and there's nowhere else to shelter.

And any time I'm around people for too long...

I've apparently been silent for too long, because Kovan bows at the waist and says, "I know it is an imposition and that I have nothing to offer you in return. I will do my best to learn quickly so that I won't be a burden—"

"Oh, whoa, no, I'm not worried about that," I assure him. "Everyone needs help sometimes. It's just... never mind. Yes, of course you can stay with me."

Awesome, good job thinking that through, self, love an impulse decision with terrifying consequences.

I stand abruptly, dusting my hands of this conversation, but Kovan stands with me and takes my hands in his.

I stand shock-still.

Someone is *touching* me. Voluntarily.

"Please." His gold eyes are mesmerizing. "Tell me."

I open my mouth to blurt it out but instead say, "Is this your sage power?"

Immediately, his eyes dull. "Definitely not."

Ah, shit. I sigh and decide to just get it out there. "This is what I'm worried about," I explain miserably. "You're going to get sick of dealing with me, and neither of us will have anywhere else to go."

His head cocks to the side. "Absolutely nothing in our interaction thus far has given me the impression that I would ever tire of you."

I snort. "Well, let me disabuse you of that. I say the first thing that comes to mind."

"I had noticed."

"I'll forget things you expect me to remember, and I'll say I'll do something and then will get caught up in something else and will do things a different way that you'll hate because it's not what we agreed on or common sense or whatever. And I'll short out all your magic, so dealing with me will always have a cost even beyond the rest."

I glare up at him, as if that will change how my heart is pounding.

Yes, fine, I just did the same 'make them hate you in advance' tactic. I didn't recognize it by accident.

But he's still holding my hands.

Now he squeezes them.

"The latter isn't a problem," Kovan says slowly, "and I admit I find it difficult to imagine that any of the rest will be, either. But I believe that you are speaking from a place of experience, and I will endeavor not to contribute to those lessons."

Well. That's something, I guess?

"You don't believe me," he says, letting my hands go.

Damn it.

Double damn it, even—for being the one to make him deflate like that, and for losing that brief—but not as brief as it should have been—connection with him.

I want it back.

All of it.

"Oh, I mean, I believe you mean what you're saying right now," I say hastily. "But patience for people who get distracted from important things always wanes eventually."

"Ah." His tone changes somehow. "You've been told that if you simply cared enough, or tried hard enough, you wouldn't forget?"

I stare.

The sage nods, like this makes perfect sense. "You don't strike me as careless. Some people simply don't work that way. As the sage of resolve, I would know. If I simply apply my magic to increase your determination to remember, it wouldn't help, because determination is not your problem. There are some spells for focus that have proven effective for some people—" He breaks off. "I apologize. I suppose those aren't available to you, as a null. I shouldn't have offered the possibility—"

"Are you *kidding*?" His words make me dizzy, and I drop down to the ground again. "You mean I'm not—okay maybe there is still something wrong with me, but I'm not just... weak?" The last word comes out on a whisper, and I wince at myself.

Kovan crouches in front of me, and when I meet his gaze I'm mesmerized all over again.

He may not be able to use magic right now, but his golden eyes glow with fierceness, and I'm drawn to the far more mundane—*more* magical—power in them.

Living together will definitely be fine and I will absolutely not embarrass myself constantly—

"There is nothing wrong with you," the Sage of Resolve says.

And I can very nearly believe it.

But as if he can sense that I'm still reeling, his eyes narrow.

And then he *offers* me a hand.

I want it. But do I deserve it?

"Will you tell me about this house?" he asks evenly.

A request, this time; not an interrogation. He's learning.

Maybe I can too.

I take a breath, and take his hand, and let him pull me to my feet.

His hand is solid in mine, and warmth spreads from the point of our connection all the way through me.

I stare at him, unsettled by the strength of my reaction to him. Then his eyebrows slowly climb, and I step back abruptly.

Definitely have not been touched in too long.

Maybe don't literally cling to the first person to do so in... however long it's been? Great, good plan, self.

"The house," the sage prompts in a tone I can't read yet.

Right! The house. "The Sage of Wrath's detonation—that's what we've been calling it, do the priests have another term?—Anyway, it blew out most of the spells down in the village. And there are spells in everything, right? That's how the priests keep people depend—uh. I mean, it's what priests, um, contribute to society. Out of the goodness of their hearts."

"I'm aware of taxation," Kovan says dryly.

"Okay, well, in my defense, you're not aware of cooking—"

"I'm aware that cooking *exists*—"

"—or that not teaching basic life skills is a classic abuse tactic to increase dependency—oh shit. See, now I've gone too far again."

Kovan is silent for a moment but then says quietly, "No. No, I don't think you have."

I *definitely* can't help with the crisis of faith. I rush onward as I move around the common room, folding a blanket, picking up a mug, and although he doesn't move, his gaze follows me as I flutter ineffectually around him.

"Um. So, a lot of buildings collapsed, basically, and a lot of the stuff inside them too. The spells in town are destabilized, so most people can't safely get near them, so I've been going through the wreckage to sort whatever can be repurposed and separating out anything that still has a working spell on it by moving everything around it."

"How can you tell?"

"If the spell is working? Well—"

"If it can be repurposed."

"Oh! I've um. Tried a lot of jobs, and nothing really took, but—"

"What do you mean, nothing took?" he asks sharply.

I open my mouth to answer automatically, then point at him. "Interrogating."

Kovan actually *swears*.

The sheer unexpectedness of it makes me laugh out loud.

Right up until I remember what he was asking about, and my smile fades.

The sage takes a breath. "May I ask if you were unhappy in your... previous occupation?"

I swallow, my hands clenching on the blanket I have folded and unfolded half a dozen times now like a lifeline before I finally set it down and gently pat it into place. "You may," I say lightly. "And let's say I think it was approaching its natural end point, so being able to contribute in a new way was really a boon."

More like I had been hanging on for dear life.

Like I had with every other job I've ever tried that ultimately didn't work out.

And I have tried... pretty much everything, at this point.

(Carpenter. Plumber. Seamstress. Blacksmith. Apothecary... Just. *So* many.)

I shouldn't be grateful for a magical working that has made life so much harder for all my neighbors.

But I honestly don't know what I would have done without it.

"Contributing," Kovan says flatly, "out of the goodness of your heart."

What's that supposed to mean?

"I mean, people are paying me for the salvage pieces? *But*, I had a bunch of these great pieces stacking up that no one wanted, right, and then I thought—well, everyone agrees it's too dangerous for me to touch anything still standing in town, so I thought, maybe I could just make something with them in a place that won't be in anyone's way. So that's why the cottage is here, and that's why everything is kind of mismatched, and... I haven't decided if the roof is going to be a problem, honestly, I know it's asymmetrical but I *think* it will still be fine once the snowy months hit—"

"You're telling me that in less than a month, you have changed your entire livelihood, cleaned up the aftermath of a sage's... *detonation*, alone both at the temple and amidst the destruction of your village, and assembled a house from pieces of *scrap*?"

"I mean, it's a weird house," I point out. "And most of the pieces were built already so I just had to figure a few things out to put them together—"

"You settled on an entirely new course of action without any assistance and followed through all the way."

"Yes, but that's because I got excited? It's always easier for me when something feels shiny and new."

It *still* feels shiny and new though, honestly.

Maybe because I never find two pieces that are the same, so every time I have to learn a new thing to do.

I'm trying really, really hard not to overthink it. To rely on it. Because once I do—

"You clearly do not fully appreciate how impressive this is," Kovan says, "or how rare. But I do. And if you can't believe in my knowledge as a sage, at least believe that I personally wouldn't have known where to even *start*."

"That's hardly comparable, you *do* have a job that you're a unique expert at aaand there I go again."

His shoulders droop only a little, but given what showing even that must cost the avatar of resolve makes me feel like a worm.

"I'm so sorry," I say quietly.

His lips twist bitterly. "If I had learned more than magic, you wouldn't be."

I frown. "I wouldn't apologize for hurting your feelings, even if it was an accident? That sounds bad, actually."

"You wouldn't doubt yourself every time you speak truth," he says. "I can't do even this."

It takes me a minute to work through what I think he's saying, which is that he's been trying to make me feel more assured in his presence but it hasn't magically worked in the span of a few minutes and so he's a failure.

"I think you might have unreasonable expectations for how easy it is to change people's feelings without literal magic," I say slowly. "But you definitely started."

"A start doesn't actually help you."

"Yeah, it absolutely does? Just because you can't do something all at once doesn't mean it's not worth doing?"

He snorts. "You might sound more convincing if you weren't ending those sentences with question marks."

"I don't doubt what I'm saying," I tell him. "I'm confused that I have to say it. But okay. You want to help. I hear you. Can I teach you how to make bread?"

The sage rolls his eyes at me.

He rolls his eyes!

"Did you want to help me or not?" I demand.

"By doing something you can already do?" Kovan scoffs.

"First of all, taking a burden off of someone else *is* help. Secondly, I know *how* to make bread, but I am *terrible* at it. I'm terrible at it even normally, because you have to remember to do things at certain times which is basically impossible for me, but now even though I know the oven is working because other things are cooking fine, every attempt I've made at bread on this mountain has been a *disaster* and I stopped trying. So I will teach you how to make bread, and then you will figure out how to actually make it, because *you* won't stop trying, so not only will you be able to feed yourself, you will be *helping me*."

A long pause.

"I would be happy to learn how to make bread," the sage finally says quietly.

I belatedly realize my fists are clenched, and I release them, breathing hard.

I have been yelling at a sage. At a guest in my house that I have to live with now! Argh.

Rather than open my mouth and make it worse again, I move past him to a cupboard and pull out a big book.

It's a gorgeous tome of a book, and huge, and not something even a little bit practical and I love it so unreasonably that I have been unable to bring myself to actually *do* anything with it.

Like my touch will somehow ruin its magic, too.

"I brought this here to write down all the recipe adaptations I learned and then, well, I didn't do it," I say. "So you can use it to keep track of things instead. I'll show you how to get started first."

"Thank you," he says quietly.

I want to tell him not to thank me, because once he feels able to fend for himself I won't feel guilty when our living together inevitably doesn't work out.

I want to tell him not to thank me because he shouldn't need to be grateful for someone teaching him something as basic as how to make bread.

But I don't want him to feel any worse.

I don't want him to feel like even basic kindness is a weapon that can be wielded against him.

I refuse to pass that on if I can possibly help it.

I refuse to let how other people treat me make me like them. Make me *hard*, when what I really want is to be able to be excited about anything and not have to feel bad about it.

So he can have my beautiful book.

And all I say is, "You're welcome."

Despite what I said before, his touch then, gently covering my hands as I work the dough, his steady gaze focused intently on a task he's not even interested in but is caring about for my sake, does start to make me believe that maybe he does, in fact, mean everything he says.

Even about me.

CHAPTER 3

KOVAN

For the remainder of the morning, Tasa teaches me everything she knows about bread, and it is the easiest thing in the world to focus all my attention on *her*, and her brightness.

Her brown eyes and hair catch the light as she smiles, which she does easily and often, as she moves, not gracefully but in bursts of energy.

I hadn't realized that easy excitement was something missing in my life until this moment. Being a sage isn't about joy, so it isn't necessary; but it's certainly not present.

The sage of resolve is about bringing determination in hard situations. Battles. The aftermaths of disasters. Difficult and massive undertakings. Digging deep and drawing on inner mettle.

There can be triumph, or a kind of fierce group determination, but I'm never called on for *joy*. The priests around me, likewise, are serious in their dedication.

Tasa is dazzling with it. And watching her unlocks a yearning in me I am completely unprepared for and absolutely cannot touch.

Being in her presence feels like basking in sunshine. Like she brings a lightness into the room with her, like everything is more possible, and the thoughts weighing on me don't feel so heavy.

The last thing I want is to bring her bright energy down.

If my learning how to bake bread will ease her spirit—and the strain my presence will bring—then I will, of all the things I can't imagine for myself, bake bread.

For someone who can't do it herself, the depth and breadth of Tasa's knowledge is remarkable, but she resists any attempt to acknowledge that.

As though curiosity about the world is not remarkable on its own, and it is only through practical results that she can have value.

And I understand that way of thinking too well. My failure—unwillingness or inability, either way the result is the same—to work magic on the scale of the Sage of Wrath's tremendous dampening field has made me feel useless.

But in Tasa, who clearly has so much *more* to offer the world, this bothers me.

So I'm thinking about it.

I don't have any answers yet, but I am thinking.

For all the good it has done me so far. What I need is to act, but I don't know how.

The only inkling my own brain has offered up since meeting Tasa is a yearning for more than basking in her joy: participating in it, *touching* it; touching *her*. I banish the thought, stilling with an act of will the unexpected urge to reach for her as it continues cropping up like a twitch, because this is not one it is in any way appropriate to pursue even if I knew how.

I am a guest in Tasa's house, but not a welcome one, and I don't dare make this situation more awkward.

My own thoughts are too mixed in any case, so I will do what Tasa wants.

Bake bread.

And no more.

Bake bread, and not touch her any more than necessary, or stare at her like her face contains the answers to any question I might ask, or ask her everything I want to know about her.

Listen to her words, and what she does not say so that I may fill in the gaps. Focus on how she moves, that I might move with her and not against her.

That is what is available to me.

But after I have mixed the bread dough, waited the precise recommended time, and added more starter, Tasa leaves to hike back down the mountain, and my abrupt tension when she announces this takes us both by surprise.

Apparently she hikes up and down this mountain twice each day in order to not be in the way of the villagers.

This bothers me too. A great deal.

But I recognize that people do what they must to make money, and if she believes this is the best way to do it, who am I to gainsay her?

So while she is gone, I wait.

I've committed all her instructions to memory, so first I write them all down in the book she provided.

It's a gorgeous tome. It feels wrong to use it for something so mundane.

Then again: how to live may be mundane, but it is also, in a way, the most important question a person faces.

I fold the bread.

Tasa told me to explore the cottage while she was out, so that's next. She seems to be both proud and embarrassed by it and was too nervous to show me herself. I can't deny that I'm curious why.

The main room contains both the kitchen, the cozier section where we talked which is for, I assume, relaxing, and a small dining table in between to break up each space. She has laid out the room with an economical efficiency I admire.

There are wings on each side with more rooms. On one side there is a workshop with a slab of wood repurposed as a table and a sturdy chair, while the rest is full of tools, slabs, and trinkets and all kinds of things I can't even identify.

But all things that Tasa has seen potential in and collected.

I wonder, wryly, if she would include me among them.

Imagining the keenness in her gaze as she fixates on a new idea makes my lips curve.

Imaging that same gaze at seeing me in here... I banish the thought with a scowl, my good humor dropping away.

She is not for one such as me to want.

Not a man in *hiding*, who has nothing to offer.

Not a failure of a sage.

A sage might have much to offer to the world, in theory.

But not to a person.

At least, not a sage such as I am.

In fact it strikes me that I can't sense any magic whatsoever in this workshop. I have no idea if that's because of the magic dampening field, or because of her nullifying powers.

What an absolute marvel. If the priesthood were smart, they'd have recruited her long since—just imagine how useful she could be in a battle of magic.

This idea bothers me too, now—not just because of how I am now thinking about the value of *usefulness*, but also because I find that I would not trust the priesthood with her, and given that I have spent my entire life being useful to them, that is damning—of me or them, I'm not yet sure.

Perhaps both.

But I gather that instead Tasa has spent her life as a kind of pariah, and I'm not sure if that is better or worse, only that I hate it.

There appears to be no particular organization in this room, so I bring the load in that she left outside in her worry for Zan. This, at least, I can do.

The load is heavier than I expected. Sages train daily, but Tasa has been carrying weights up a mountain.

And apparently thinks nothing of it, compared to the prospect of living near her neighbors.

That is also damning.

I fold the bread.

On the other side of the main living area are two rooms, a bedroom and a bathroom: a toilet, a sink, and the largest bathtub I've ever seen, which fills me with unexpected, fierce pride for her.

If she feels she can't be comfortable elsewhere, if she has to live alone and build her own house and hike a mountain twice a day, then she *deserves* a comfort this extravagant, and I love that she has taken it for herself.

Even if she's embarrassed by it.

Someday, the thought comes to me, I want her to feel that she can show it, and her ingenuity, off with pride.

It's not quite resolve, because I don't know how to make that happen, if *I* even can.

But it's a thing I *want* to feel resolve about, and right now, that is a gift.

The bedroom is fairly bare—no surprise, as she hasn't even quite finished building the house, let alone had time to decorate.

There is a single pot of dirt that I stare at for too long, wondering if I should water it; how to know.

And there is space for more, but what strikes me is that there is only one bed.

I banish *those* thoughts too, disgusted with myself.

Perhaps this is why she was nervous to tell me about her home, and I will *not* validate her fears.

There. *That* is resolve: an action I feel strongly about and that will require my active commitment to make come to pass.

Not simply to rein myself in, but to pay attention to her cues, to do whatever is necessary so that I do not contribute to her feelings of discomfort in her own home.

My presence at all is an obstacle to that, so I must mitigate it.

It occurs to me that Tasa feeling she has to mitigate her presence among her neighbors bothers me, but this is different. It is. Sages are different.

I banish the thought and focus on the task at hand.

Discipline I can do.

There's plenty of space to sleep on the floor, which I can do too. Not happily—my bones aren't young enough for that anymore—but it's been a recurring part of my training.

But I find a small closet with extra blankets—*lots* of extra blankets, which makes me wonder just how cold it will get at night, and decide I can take a page from Tasa's book and build something: a pallet on the floor.

Then again—would Tasa find this intrusive, having me sleep in her bedroom? Or would it be more intrusive for me to sleep in her sitting room, pressuring her not to make noise when she returns home hungry? To sleep in her workshop, so she can't freely use her time to pursue the many interests in her mind?

Ultimately I decide the floor of her bedroom is the best option. My pile of blankets still looks intrusive, and somehow out of place even in this house where everything is, in theory, out of place, but all the rest of it fits somehow.

I don't have a place with her. Even if I have forced myself into her world, seized a corner of her space.

I fold the bread.

It's afternoon now, and I go to eat the cheese and cured meats Tasa left out for me. Apparently predicting that I would tell her I could go without—she was not, after all, prepared for a house "guest"—she informed me that food is most often what she is traded for her labor and that she has more than she can eat before it goes bad.

This bothers me, too.

I'm glad that she isn't in danger of going hungry, of course.

But why should she have to accept food that she doesn't need, if she might need something else? Blankets apparently are plentiful, but what if she needs new boots or a coat? What if she wants a new, beautiful book for herself, but has no currency? If she is performing necessary labor, why should she not have the same ability as any other villager to acquire for herself whatever *she* chooses?

On the heels of that thought, another, more dangerous follows: Why should she have to perform labor to deserve to have enough food?

I fold the bread.

According to Tasa's instructions, now I need to leave the dough to ferment for hours before touching it again.

I'm out of tasks to fill my hands.

In the silence of the empty mountain, my uselessness creeps back in relentlessly.

As I clean the sticky dough from my hands, only now does it occur to me to wonder how she has running water on the side of a mountain with no magic, and I resolve to ask.

There, that's something I can do. I can ask questions.

Tasa said that taking people's burdens on can be a true help, and the gods know I would rather take hers than mine right now.

After a brief internal debate—am I really going to fill the book with even *more* mundane thoughts? Then again, perhaps these questions are also about how to live—I bring the book with me to my pile of blankets.

Where I will, I hope, intrude the least on a generous woman who clearly doesn't want me here, and who can blame her?

I write questions like:

What can I do to make my presence here less of a burden?
May I organize your workshop?
How did you do all this without magic?
What would you trade for if not food?

What do you need to live?
I stare at those words again.
What do you need to live?
Something about them strikes a deep chord inside me.

But emotional, magical—and perhaps existential—exhaustion from the events of the day so far sneak up on me. And with a full stomach and nothing to do to focus my resolve on, sleep takes me.

W<small>HEN</small> I <small>WAKE</small>, <small>THE</small> world is dark.

Disoriented, I lie still, taking a moment to feel the blankets beneath me, to remember where I am.

And on the tail of that, to remember *why* I'm here.

It comes crashing down on me, a weight settling on my chest and holding me down.

I can't simply sleep my responsibilities away. *That* was weakness. And yet, facing the enormity of what I've done again, alone in the darkness—I try to breathe through it.

And in so doing, I hear the sound of other breath.

Tasa.

Maybe I can sit up after all.

My eyes adjust—it's nighttime, but there's a window letting through just enough moonlight that I can see, first, that she has covered me with more blankets, which arrests me.

It's not that no one has ever been concerned with my comfort. But this feels different. Not someone trying to maintain the health of an asset, just... care.

I move quietly so as not to disturb her and find her sleeping peacefully in her bed.

Part of the weight on my chest eases.

At least I haven't disturbed her peace so much that she can't still find it here, with me in her home, in her *room*.

But she has many fewer blankets than I do—which seems typical for her, to concern herself with others' comfort before her own, but nevertheless not acceptable—so I gently drape some of the ones she gave me over her instead.

Her breath hitches, and I freeze. *Did I try to help and make everything worse, ruining a fragile peace after all—*

And then she relaxes, burrowing into the greater warmth.

I take a breath.

And when I let it out, I make myself back away—before I can disturb her in truth—and creep out into the main room.

I'm awake, and I don't know what else to do, but Tasa tasked me with making bread, and if that is the *one* thing I can do, then I ought to at least *do it*.

As I wait for the bread to bake before starting another batch, I finally realize that the beautiful book is open on the table.

I'd seen it, but now I make the connection that it had still been on my lap when I'd fallen asleep, which means Tasa must have moved it.

And may have seen more of myself than I have allowed anyone to before—perhaps even myself.

With a mix of anticipation and fear, I slowly make my way to the book.

The first thing I notice is her drawing of a smiling face.

She's not even awake, but that weight lifts off of me nevertheless.

Tasa has left little notes of encouragement—hearts and stars and comments on my bread notes that make me smile.

And then I see that she found my questions, and answered them, too.

My heart pounds as I read them.

You're not a burden.

No qualification. I swallow.

Actually yes, organizing my workshop would be great if you really don't mind? I know you probably don't know what a lot of stuff is, but also I genuinely do not know where anything is, so.

I think you may be underestimating what people can do without magic?

I got you some pants! And a shirt. I hope that's okay, I don't actually know ~~what's underneath your robes~~ *what you like but thought you might not want to wear the same clothes every day?*

I have to squint to make out the words she attempted to cross out, and they make my lips curve in amusement.

Probably I should be bothered that she answered my question about what she wants with a gift for *me*, but then again, that is perhaps its own answer.

I didn't ask what she wanted for herself, after all.

And I *am* bothered that this must mean she forewent payment for her labor to take care of me.

But mostly I'm—perhaps smug? that she is thinking about whether I wear pants.

Then I see her last answer, and my smile fades.

I'm not sure if this one is actually a question for me, but just in case: I think something small to hold onto.

What do you need to live? I'd asked.

As a sage, I should be the one able to answer that question. When I wrote it, I meant something more basic.

But her answer—the answer of a person without divine power—is more fundamental still.

I sit with that for a few minutes until the bread is done.

The bread collapsed.

Tasa warned me this had been happening to her since she moved here, but she tasked *me* with figuring out how to fix it.

Something small to hold onto.

A pot of dirt.

It's time to start figuring out how I will.

CHAPTER 4

TASA

I WAKE BEFORE DAWN, warm and disinclined to move. But as the light starts emerging, I'll be able to see enough to get down the mountain and do my work. I really should move.

I roll over with my pile of blankets to hold onto this drowsy ease for another minute—I'm still getting used to the unanticipated relief of not having to worry about how I'll affect anyone else's schedule—and see that Kovan is still sleeping at my feet.

Well, abandoning your entire life with no safety net is a big choice; I'm not surprised he needed to rest.

It doesn't look like it is an easy one, though. His brows are furrowed even in sleep, his jaw clenched, and my chest tightens.

I guess this can't be his haven after all.

I didn't want anyone in my space, so it's unreasonable for me to be disappointed that being here doesn't magically make him as happy as it's made me.

Then I notice that the blankets I put on him are gone, and frown.

For a second I think I messed up—everyone always tells me I'm too much, that I should stay out of their way, but it gets *cold* here at night and I don't think it was ridiculous to think that a sage might not realize *how* cold—

And then I realize he didn't just take them off, he put them on *me*.

I blink back sudden, stupid tears as warmth fills me.

The sage—*Kovan*—is trying to take care of me. Like he is with the bread. Like he is with this pile of blankets on the floor when obviously he should have just taken the bed instead and I'd have slept on the couch, but it seemed silly for neither of us to use the bed so I'd done it anyway after finding him.

Still. He woke up long enough to see what I'd done for him and decide to do something for me instead.

When was the last time someone cared?

Wow, depressing question, and what a great reason to get myself out of bed so I stop thinking about it.

I tiptoe to the kitchen and find that the man also apparently woke up long enough to bake a whole loaf of bread in the middle of the night?

I can't believe I didn't hear, honestly. I *like* being up here, but I'm still getting used to all the sounds, and I normally wake up in the night a few times.

But I slept all the way through this.

Was it the extra warmth? Or the warmth from knowing a person was with me, trying not to encroach on *me* for once?

My chest tightens again. I knew it would be hard to have him here, and then for him to leave. But a sage is too important for someone like me.

Even if he baked bread for me.

The important part is that he did it! Kovan cooked something for the first time, all by himself.

He's so going to be fine without me.

That combination of pride and despair stays with me all the way down the mountain.

When I get back, the door to my cottage flies open before I'm even close, and Kovan advances on me.

The first thing I notice is that he's taken off his robes, and wow is he even more attractive this way than I was expecting.

He's wearing the pants that I brought for him. They fit—which isn't the biggest surprise because, despite the robes, one of the many jobs I've tried was seamstress—but, gods, do they *fit*.

And with the background of my cottage behind him, dressed like a normal person, he looks... maybe not attainable.

But *touchable*.

Dangerous thoughts.

And as he closes in, my breath catches at the determined light in his golden eyes.

Being the focus of that intensity is... *wow*.

Then he reaches for my load. "I can carry this inside."

I step back, startled out of the very inappropriate direction my daydreams were taking. *Stop that. He has nowhere else to go.* "I don't need you to?"

His golden gaze fixates on mine, almost like he's angry? For what, carrying my own stuff? Being denied?

My heart pounds, and I'm not sure any more what emotion is causing it. My awareness was already heightened, but I think now we've been dropped without warning into a different kind of tension.

"You told me that lightening burdens is real help," Kovan says tightly.

Okay, breathing. I was not prepared for our second meeting to be as confrontational as the first, especially following my maybe over-the-top reaction to seeing him in different clothes that I chose for him so that's even my own fault.

But I *am* used to people attacking me without apparent warning, and I lift my chin.

The sage's eyes widen.

What, did he think I would just roll over when he started making demands of me?

I mean, honestly that would be more logical. He's a goddamn *sage*.

But I keep my tone even like I always do when this happens.

Making people mad a lot has made me good in a crisis, at least.

"It can be, yes," I say, "but I'm also not helpless. *You* made me think that I wasn't weak."

That comes out more accusingly than I meant it to.

Kovan freezes.

And then says fiercely, "You're *not*."

Then what is his *problem*?

I don't even know what I'm feeling now, but it's definitely not any less complicated than when I left.

"Great. Then I can manage my own shit. The difference, to be clear, is that it's not helping if you're pushing yourself where you're not wanted."

"Damn it," he mutters.

Okay, that was... easier than I expected, honestly. But my hackles are still raised—I can't quite believe that someone is just going to accept me.

"Are you bored of bread already?" I ask lightly, trying to figure out what in the world brought this on. Not the desire to help, but the—ahh, there it is.

Kovan scowls. "I wanted to have bread ready for you when you got home, but it's bad."

Oh. That's... sweet, sort of, except that he accidentally took it out on me. But he stopped as soon as I pointed it out and actually told me what the problem was, which is... way better than how this usually goes for me, honestly, and obscurely finally eases my tension.

We make it to the door, and Kovan asks, "Will you leave these things here for now? I can sort them into the workshop."

"Oh, wow, you've already done that?"

He scowls harder. "No. It's taking longer than anticipated. I've made a mess of your space."

I can tell he's really upset about this so I manage to hold back my laugh but kind of wish I'd been here to watch a sage learn about organizing.

My heart is still beating rapidly, but the tension is fading. Or, well, one tension. The important one, because what I might secretly want isn't.

"That's fine," I say, unloading my pack to leave at the door. "I didn't expect that to be fast. I have a *lot* of crap in there."

"It's not *crap*," Kovan snaps.

I blink. "I know?"

He takes a breath. "I apologize," he says stiffly.

I watch him for a moment and then nod, heading into the house. "Okay. You're clearly having big feelings. Let's try your bread."

He follows on my heels. "It's not—"

"Kovan!" I whirl, jabbing him in the chest. "Look at it! You got it to rise and not collapse on just your second try! That's amazing! Why in the world are you mad?"

"Because it still *tastes* bad," he tells me testily. "You gave me *one* task—"

"—which I have *struggled* with and in no way expected you to resolve in one day having *literally never cooked before*—"

"—I have *one way* to ease the burden I am placing on you, and I tried another and that *also* has made things worse for you—"

"I'm really surprised that a sage of resolve seems to think that things are only worthwhile if they're done immediately? There isn't a time limit on figuring out how to make bread."

"I *resolved*," Kovan practically snarls, "to not add further burden to *you*, and I have done *the exact opposite*."

I grab his face in my hands, which seems to short-circuit his brain.

It will probably short-circuit mine too if I stop to think about what I'm doing for longer than a second, so I don't.

"Kovan, look at me. This morning I got to eat bread in my own home for the first time in weeks. *You made bread.* And then you made *better* bread. Two whole loaves! Do you have any idea how many batches I've had to scrap because I flat out forgot about them? As far as I'm concerned, right now you're made of magic, and not the sage kind. I don't even remember what's in the ice house, Kovan."

He frowns. "Is it not ice?"

I open my mouth; close it. "I mean, there is also ice, which is now going to have to last a lot longer, but that's not the point. The *point* is that you are being unreasonably hard on yourself—no, don't argue with me, are you going to stand there and tell me that if *I* had baked that bread my first time that you'd be giving me shit about it?"

Kovan closes his mouth.

"Yeah, that's what I thought."

He... keeps staring at me.

Oops, still holding his face in my hands. I yank them back like they're too close to the fire—and maybe, given what kind of heat he makes me feel, they are.

Something flashes in his gaze, but I'm already turning away so my flush isn't as obvious.

Then I turn back and inform him, "I'm going to eat a piece."

A muscle in his jaw ticks, but he nods.

I cut a piece for me, and one for him.

Kovan's gaze is intent on mine as I take a bite, making me blush for reasons I don't fully understand. I'm eating *bread*, for gods' sake.

Once I swallow, I raise my eyebrows. "Are you going to eat too, or just watch me?"

"It's bad."

"Who knew sages were so picky?" I tease. "So hard, not having your life fully catered to."

Kovan narrows his eyes at me.

Then he stuffs a bite in his mouth.

Ha, got him. And judging by the way his gaze never leaves mine, he knows it.

"And it's not great *yet*," I correct him. "Too dense. What did you change?"

He swallows and says tightly, "Added more yeast."

"Okay, so that helped the structure but not the texture. You learned something! What are you trying next? I assume you didn't just give up?"

"Of course not. I'm changing the amount of water."

"Oh, good idea. And, honestly, the flavor might be my fault—I don't remember to feed the starter regularly. So it'll only get better now that it's under your control."

There's a long pause.

Finally Kovan says, his voice wry, "I think I may need to learn how to be useful even when I'm not in control."

I freeze while taking another bite of bread.

Very deliberately, I swallow.

"Or at least," the sage sighs, "learning how to not accidentally cause problems."

"Well, that I definitely can't help with," I say. "But I would also... maybe not recommend wanting to be useful to people first and foremost?"

Kovan's eyebrows draw down. "That sounds... at odds with how I have lived thus far. Can you say more? You don't want to be useful to people?"

Whoops accidentally waded into the faith crisis. Crap.

"Oh, no, I definitely do, that's exactly it. But one reason I wanted to be up here so badly was to have a place where it was safe to be *me*, you know?"

And I'm not sure I do have that place anymore.

I mean, I can actually talk to him, and he doesn't get mad at what I say or do, and he acknowledges his faults and explains himself.

I slept easily with him next to me.

But sooner or later—and my experience always points to sooner—he's going to get frustrated with how frivolous I am next to his intensity.

And once that happens, and he leaves, I'm not sure this will still feel like my haven.

KOVAN

THE IDEA OF LIVING to *not* be useful feels like such an attack on my identity that I know I'm going to need to think more about why, and what that means.

The idea of wanting a place to just be myself—*that* is entirely foreign to me. It's not *possible*. I am a sage; there's no separating that from my identity. The power was mine before the priests took me in.

But if I don't know who I am if I'm not being of service, perhaps that is the crux of my problem.

Right now, there is only a single person next to me that I *must* find a way to help, and it is damning that I can't figure out how.

Why is it harder to think about how to help just Tasa than to do work on a grander scale?

In my partial defense, I can't use magic, which is how I usually solve problems. And I'm usually only directed at problems that resolve can help with.

But since I am the vessel of divinity—which hasn't changed, and I have made it my life's work to study the manifestation of resolve that I am the channel for—it is damning that without magic, my ability to help her feel more secure in herself is so lacking.

"How can you be yourself here where you can't in Crystal Hollow?" I ask.

"Oh boy. That's a complicated question." Tasa takes another bite of my inferior bread, not giving any sign that she doesn't enjoy it.

My chest tightens, and I'm not sure why.

"The simplest answer," she says, "is that I don't have to worry about breaking things up here. Not only am I alone—I mean, before you got here anyway—"

Another way I am adding to her burdens, though I can't help but add, "And Zan."

"Yes, but Zan doesn't *stay*. So I don't have to worry about being in his way, right? At least not all the time."

"How can you be in someone's way in your own house?"

Tasa huffs and mutters, "You'd be surprised. What I was getting at is that I can't nullify anything important up here. No accidentally breaking the means of someone's livelihood. I've had to fix all my appliances for years because the spells would inevitably go out, so up here, since I don't have to be connected to the spells that keep magical energy flowing, I can just build a house designed for *me*. I don't have to tiptoe around my own house worrying about which of my neighbors I'm going to hurt."

Hurt seems like a strong word, but part of me grasps her meaning anyway.

Not the same, of course—sages don't literally break things.

But when I walk into a room, conversation stops.

I have to be careful about what I say, what I do, because people are always watching.

If I am not the picture of resolution at all times, their own resolve wanes.

It's a weight. One it is an honor to carry—can I truly complain that people pay attention when I speak?—but it does mean that I am always judged.

And from what Tasa has said, I suspect no one places any weight on *her* words.

Another piece of what she said catches my interest, though, so I move away from the questions that clearly make her more uncomfortable, when that wasn't actually what I was going for.

Sages are *supposed* to cause ripples; it's a hard habit to break.

"If you can't be connected to the magical spell network up here, how do you have plumbing?"

Tasa lets out a crack of laughter. "I take it you don't know anything about plumbing?"

I narrow my eyes. "I take it you do."

"Yeah," she laughs again. "You could say that. People don't need magic to have plumbing, Kovan. I mean, magic can help get it set up, but once the pipes are in, they just need maintenance. Usually spells take care of that too, but since I've been nullifying spells my entire life I have also learned... way more than anyone wants to know about plumbing."

It strikes me, then, that *I* want to know.

Not about plumbing specifically.

I want to know what her life is like.

I want to see her excited to share all her copious knowledge rather than rueful.

I thought I knew where I stood in the world, and I am coming to the realization that I may not even know what the world is.

"So what you're telling me," I say, "is that in addition to clearing dangerous magical debris from your village and building an entire house, you have also, *within the last month*, fixed the failed temple plumbing system on the side of a mountain."

"You say that like I did that out of the goodness of my heart," Tasa says. "I very much got a personal benefit from it."

This, with her, I already understand. "Oh? And did you charge your neighbors to fix their plumbing systems?"

"Of course not. I'm the one who broke them!"

"And if they couldn't afford a plumber, or asked if you would mind just dropping by to take a look at something, did you also volunteer free labor?"

Tasa's eyes narrow. "Of course I did. There's nothing wrong with helping people."

"There's something wrong with people taking advantage of you, Tasa."

She points at me with yet another piece of bread. "First of all, even if I was a mean person and didn't want to help my neighbors, as a null there is a practical utility in my neighbors being kindly disposed toward me since I'm inevitably going to fuck up their lives by existing near them."

"You shouldn't have to pay an extra tithe simply to live in a society," I snap.

"Well, I do," Tasa snaps back, "and that's why I live alone on a mountain now. And while you're getting in a snit about me, tell me, when have *you* ever asked for anything for yourself?"

I pause.

She crosses her arms and glares.

"That's different," I say.

Tasa scoffs.

"The temple has provided for all my needs my entire life—"

"Debatable, but what about your wants?"

"I'm a divine vessel," I grit out.

And then remember how Zan reacted to that argument.

Tasa's not any more impressed with it. "You're also a person!"

"A sage has a unique way to be useful to society as a whole, that is *why* your taxes cover our care—"

"Your care or your upkeep?"

I start to answer.

Then remember my frustration that Tasa doesn't choose her form of payment.

On the edge of an epiphany.

"Being born a null doesn't define my profession," Tasa bulls onward. "And even though I know about plumbing I'm not *required* to be a plumber, right? Like, maybe I should be. People definitely told me to, and I tried, I did. Fixing things is fun, but fixing the same thing every day is depressing as shit to me. Do you even like doing sage work? Have you ever tried anything else?"

Another question I have simply never asked. That no one else has dared ask me, either, because what was the point?

But Tasa, a person with no divine mandate or training, is asking.

The kind of disruptive question that a sage should ask.

"I do like doing sage work," I say slowly.

But as I feel my way through that answer, I realize I am less sure that I like being a sage.

I can't quite wrap my head around that, let alone speak the words aloud, as if they'll make the notion more real.

So instead I continue, "But no, I have not tried anything else. However, as you aptly pointed out, I do not know anything about plumbing, or anything else practical in a place without magic."

My voice comes out a little more bitterly than I expected.

"It's not *no* magic though, right?" Tasa points out. "Because it's magic that keeps you from doing magic."

"A place with magic so strong that it prevents the strongest remaining sage from doing magic," I say dryly. "That's much better."

She throws her bread crust at me.

Stunned, I let it hit me.

It bounces to the floor.

Tasa shakes with laughter.

"My point," she manages between breaths, "is that there *is* still magic, and you know spells, right? The thing that Crystal Hollow is currently in dire need of, since no priests are willing to risk being powerless to come help? Some magic still works at the base of the mountain, albeit inconsistently. You specifically *could* actually help people in a practical way by doing sage work."

I blink.

Blink again.

"A nice thought," I say, "but sages are rarely called upon to participate in spellwork, and in those cases it's only for very specific, serious workings. I know more principles than anything else. I wouldn't know how to set up a plumbing system."

"We don't need fancy things. Crystal Hollow already has plumbing, remember? Principles might be enough."

I frown, considering that as I turn away and begin to knead the dough again.

"If you don't like that idea, that's fine," Tasa says. "I didn't want to be a plumber, remember. It's just an idea."

I already knew, but her need to justify makes it clear that it is not, in fact, just an idea.

"It's an idea that makes me feel both more and less useful," I explain. "Most of what I can do, what I excel at, *is* what you would call the fancy things. And I think what is meaningful to me about the work of a sage is the ability to do work on a grand scale. So trying to instead do something small—to figure out *how* to do small things, and—" I gesture ineffectually at the dough now coating my hands. "—failing, feels like... not enough. Or not..."

"Worthy of a sage?" Tasa asks.

I glance at her sidelong, expecting to see judgment, but she only looks thoughtful, so I nod, a quick jerk.

My identity *is* inextricably tied to being a sage. I don't think I *want* to separate it.

If anything, I want to be *more* of a sage, because since the Sage of Wrath's detonation, I've come to believe that I am less.

"Well," Tasa finally says, "I am for sure not an expert in living a worthwhile life, but I do know it's better to do something than nothing. And if you're already moving, it's easier to keep moving. So you might as well start with something small, where it'll be easier, and see where that takes you."

"I don't think small *will* be easier for me," I mutter, "which perhaps supports your point that I will learn something useful from it. But it doesn't change that I *should* be able to do big things. Especially since I could—or I could have before I came to this place—if—"

If I had the resolve.

If I knew what to do.

"Do you know what to do, though?" Tasa asks.

No judgment in her tone; just query, as though she's one of the Learneds who trained me, but with her there's no wrong answer.

It's like her gaze sees through me—sees *me*, like no one else has, never so clearly.

And it occurs to me that this is also, perhaps, part of what she means by wanting a space to be herself.

She meant being alone, but to me, who has effectively been alone while surrounded by people my whole life, being *with* someone who sees me, and *isn't* judging me—

That's a wholeness I've never experienced until this moment.

"If not," Tasa says into my reeling thoughts, "then you might as well try something small while you figure it out. In fairness, I have never figured it out, but I believe you can!"

That gets an unexpected laugh from me, erupting like a crack in her cozy home.

It apparently catches Tasa off guard, too, because her mouth falls open slightly.

And perhaps that's valid, because I'm honestly not sure when I last laughed.

Sages are expected to be serious.

You're also a person.

I wash my hands.

When I finish, Tasa has stepped way back, and that makes me frown again.

I want her close.

Sages live alone.

"Well, whatever you decide, I promise to cheer for you from my mess!" she chirps.

"Your *mess*?" I echo incredulously. "Do you mean the cottage you built by yourself that's absolutely perfect for you, and has been a haven for a sage having a midlife crisis? Or do you mean *my* mess, since I've arrived and intruded on your serenity and made a literal mess of your workshop?"

"My workshop was already a mess, in fairness."

"*Tasa.*"

Her eyes go wide at the rumble of my voice saying her name; her cheeks flare with pink.

And *that* makes my eyes narrow for an entirely different reason.

I am a sage. I am intruding on her home. These facts have not changed.

But if she is watching me the way I am watching her...

Then nothing. That's not my place.

Still, some part of me tightens in readiness.

"I just meant," Tasa says quickly, "if you need more space to think—"

"That demonstrably hasn't helped me."

"Well, if I'm ever in your way—"

"You," I practically growl, "are the only thing I know is solid."

Tasa laughs, but I hear the hysterical note in it. "Oh gods, you're a *sage*, surely you can tell that I am the *least* solid—"

"I am a sage, and I literally couldn't have survived a night on this mountain on my own, and here you are thriving by *yourself*. I *am* a sage, Tasa, and I *do not say things I do not mean*."

Tasa stares, clearly flummoxed by my vehemency.

I've made her speechless.

While I never want to silence her, cutting through her doubts—that *does* make me feel as if I have finally managed to do a very big thing indeed.

There is wisdom in her words. Perhaps starting with something small will lead to something big.

Perhaps starting with her is the real precipice.

"Perhaps," I say, watching closely for her reactions, "once you have eaten, and rested—or once you've completed your other work for the day, would you be willing to show me some other things I should know in order to live?"

Her cheeks flare again before she swallows, and a surge of satisfaction fills me.

"I'd love to," she says breathlessly. Then swallows and tries again, "I mean, I can take today off."

I feel my expression moving into a frown; wonder when this became such an easy default for me. "Won't that mean you won't get food?"

"Oh that's right, I haven't told you about the ice house yet! I mean, yes, I do need to work to get food, but I have plenty now and most of it won't keep. The junk in the village *will* though. I don't have to keep a specific schedule—"

A marvel.

What is it like, to have the freedom to decide what you do with your day? With all your days?

I shy away from the prospect; the responsibility of it.

But part of me also yearns for it.

"—And it's not like anyone is going to miss me," Tasa explains.

I can't believe that. Or rather: I can believe her. And I have seen humans at their lowest. Intellectually, I understand what she's saying.

But in my gut, the place where my power comes from, I can't believe it.

I debate what I want to say, because it may change things. I am a deliberate person. I *don't* say things I don't mean, and I think she's beginning to believe me.

But ultimately, I simply can't let this stand.

"I would," I tell her softly.

Her eyes brighten, and that's enough.

It's worthwhile, because *she* is worthwhile.

It's a start.

CHAPTER 5

KOVAN

The morning is precious; precarious.

After storing Tasa's latest haul in the workshop—which, when I open the door, gives her a glimpse of the disaster I've made of it and she falls over laughing at me, which is a new and unexpectedly charming experience—I remind Tasa she wanted to tell me about the ice house, and she shows me: a small stone building near the temple.

She's lucky, she says, that it wasn't simply attached to Celestial Sanctuary, or she wouldn't be able to access it. And it has huge stores of food from the expected upkeep of dozens of priests.

Dozens of priests, dead instantly at a sage's hand.

Is that the kind of grand work I want to do?

On the other hand, is it enough to water a single plant?

The spells on the ice house are broken, but it will work anyway for much of the year; the real problem is that there's no way to replenish the ice, because the system to bring ice from the top of the mountain down requires multiple people, and she—and now I—aren't enough to make it work.

Some works require more people.

I know this, intellectually, but between Tasa's unending knowledge and my being accustomed to solving problems singlehandedly, it feels like a blow.

But there's no sage power in the world—determination or wrath or joy or ingenuity—that can substitute for the simple need for more hands working on a problem.

A humbling reminder.

I bring out the massive book to note down what *is* in the ice house, since Tasa can't remember, and then we retreat back to the coziness of her cottage. As we sit next to each other on her couch—very carefully not touching, though the warmth of her, at my side, is impossible to put out of my mind—she tells me how long each food will last and from that she takes me through working out a plan for what to cook based on what needs to be eaten first, and what will need supplementing.

It's a fascinating puzzle, and one I have a very limited understanding of. The priests take care of all my food, but more than that, they can use spells to preserve food, spells that apparently most people can't afford. So food that I've been able to eat year-round simply isn't accessible to Tasa.

More than *that*, though, is the more visceral understanding of how the labor of other people to see to my base needs is what truly enabled me to grow into my power; to have the space to.

Of course Tasa has had to learn to act where I have had space to think. She, and most people, have no choice. We all do our work, but *they* must also think about where their meals will come from and how and fix their plumbing and all the facets of living in this world that have been smoothed for me.

What do you need to live?

Tasa's answer to me was simple, but I'm beginning to think wryly that in fact it's a very long list.

"So the problem with this for *me*," Tasa says, "is that I'm not going to remember the plan."

I nod. "But you can bring the list with you."

"I mean, yes, but first I would have to remember the list before I get halfway down the mountain."

I smile at her candor. "What if I keep it updated and then put it in your coat pocket every evening?"

We both pause for a moment, staring at each other.

That implies a level of intimacy—and longevity—that I don't think either of us are prepared to consider.

After a moment, Tasa, as always, smooths over my bumbling attempts to converse like a normal person. "That might help," she says ruefully, "but it wouldn't make me remember to look at the list when I'm actually acquiring food."

I can't help it.

I laugh.

"Oh, shut up!" she grumbles cheerfully, shoving me.

I grin back at her, impossibly delighted that she has touched me. That a person—that *Tasa*—is laughing. With *me*.

"Then I suppose," I say, "we will have some creative meals in our future."

Her head tilts as she studies me. "You really mean that," she says, as though considering. "Oh gods, stop, you don't need to declare again that 'I'm a mighty sage and I don't say things I don't mean, earthly peon'—"

"I do *not* sound like that," I say at her exaggeratedly low voice, but my lips twitch in amusement.

"Uh huh. If you say so. But I really would have expected you to be the kind of person to get serious about *plans*."

"I suppose I am," I say, "though much of my life has involved following other people's plans." My smile falls at that. "And at any rate, a plan that doesn't take into account the realities of the people involved is a bad plan. Perhaps if I were more able to think creatively about how to use my power I wouldn't be in this situation."

Tasa takes my hand.

I still.

My entire *being* stills, focused on that point of contact.

"I'm glad you're here," she says quietly.

I can hardly breathe.

Our gazes lock on each other.

She leans toward me, and I move with her, and I am dimly and yet painfully aware of this moment we're moving toward, scarcely daring to believe that I have somehow made this happen or let this happen but nevertheless absolutely certain I am going to kiss her—

The door to the cottage bursts open.

We both spring to our feet, but I am trained to deal with threats and by default make sure she's behind me first.

On second thought, that is actually *not* my training. In a battle situation, priests would surround me so that I had time to assess the threat and do bigger work.

This is... instinct?

Only after moving do I take in the threat in front of me.

In time to see Learned Muka notice just how close I—in a common person's pants and no robes—am standing next to a beautiful woman, alone in a cozy cottage.

Now I freeze with indecision.

But Tasa exclaims, "Are you all right? Please, sit down."

She tries to duck around me to go to the Learned, but I block her, doing it instead myself.

I'm not sure why I feel like I need to protect the person who's giving me shelter now from the person who has provided shelter for me for my entire life.

Tasa's right, though—Learned Muka looks like she's going to collapse. She's a healthy woman in middle age, but right now she looks on death's door, pale and dripping with sweat, bedraggled like she faced the ordeal of a lifetime to arrive here and only barely made it.

I can sense the loss of her magic.

I help her to the couch where Tasa and I were just sitting moments ago, ignoring the weight of her gaze on me as she pants.

Meanwhile Tasa has darted to the kitchen for water and presses it into Learned Muka's shaking hands.

But the Learned doesn't acknowledge her. Doesn't even *thank* Tasa.

Learned Muka's piercing gaze never leaves mine.

"Sage Kovan," she finally rasps, with the minutest possible bow of her head.

Not "just Kovan" now.

It shouldn't feel like an accusation.

"Learned Muka," I respond neutrally. "You can't stay here. The dampening field is hurting you."

"Not you, though, it appears," Learned Muka notes.

She's right, and I'm not sure what to make of that.

I hadn't fully understood before when Tasa told me other people couldn't come up the mountain, but now I see it.

Tasa, a null, can thrive here. I feel the loss of my access to magic emotionally, but otherwise I am physically well.

Learned Muka looks as though every step to climb this mountain was an act of will that is killing her.

I wonder if Zan experienced any negative effects.

"You can't stay here," I tell Learned Muka.

"I don't intend to," she tells me. "I'm here for you. If there was a chance that dragon hadn't carried you past where our senses can reach, this was the only place you could be."

Of course. Either I was gone, or their senses were blocked.

"And you came for me," I say softly.

But then Tasa's voice sounds from behind me as she asks, "Were you in trouble after he vanished?"

I stiffen. Just because the Learned is responsible for me does not mean our relationship is so transactional. Learned Muka knows me better than anyone else alive; she practically raised me.

When the Learned doesn't even respond to the question, though, I go even stiller.

And that's before she says only to me, "I saw the scales but cannot sense the dragon. What magic prevents you from returning? I will stay as long as I must to free you."

Resolve. This is what she taught me.

But the cost in this moment does not seem worthwhile.

Especially when the extent of her resolve is for me, and not for Tasa.

Oh, I know that Tasa is in no danger here, but the Learned doesn't.

I understand that I am a valuable asset to the priesthood.

I understand that Learned Muka has a relationship with me, and a responsibility toward me, and that as she feels her body failing her, her determination can only take her so far.

She, after all, is not a sage.

Still.

Still.

"Nothing holds me here but my own limitations," I tell her carefully. "I was not prepared to take down the dampening field at the Precipice. Until I find within myself the answer to why, I will remain at Celestial Sanctuary."

Learned Muka narrows her eyes at me, her gaze flitting to Tasa and back.

As if I have been distracted from my calling by infatuation.

Infuriating, that after all our years together, she could think that of me.

More damning, that part of me wonders if she is *right*.

"And why is this a better place than with the might of the priesthood supporting you?"

Why indeed? "Because I have had the support of the priesthood my entire life, and that has not given me the answers I seek."

Learned Muka manages to bring the glass of water to her lips.

Tasa makes as if to help steady her, but I block her arm as the Learned glares.

She would consider it an insult to her determination to allow anyone to assist her now.

And following her questioning why *I* did not choose to accept help, that makes it clear that she thinks even less of me.

I cross my arms and glare at her.

We have known each other a long time. She flinches—but then immediately takes her feet.

Prepared to stand against me, to be the rock I sharpen my determination on no matter the cost.

That drains my ire right back out.

What is the *point*?

"You're giving up," she tells me.

The words land like a blow, but like the fight I wanted from Zan, they give me the gift of centering me.

"I do not *give up*," I growl.

"Do you think I was born yesterday?" Learned Muka snaps. "Where are your robes? Where is your dedication? What have you been doing—baking bread?"

Behind me, Tasa freezes.

That, with the disdain that drips from the Learned's words has me drawing up to my full height.

"I need to bake bread to live," I tell her quietly.

And because *she* knows I do not say things I don't mean, Learned Muka freezes.

And then, to my absolute shock, falls back into her seat.

"Damn it," Learned Muka mutters. "You picked a hell of a time for this."

I don't pretend to misunderstand her.

But I do crouch down in front of her as I ask, "Did I?"

She grunts.

I *am* surprised she's not fighting me on it.

And I think I may also be angry, that if she thinks making a different choice is merited, that she didn't *prepare* me. That *was* her job.

Unless there is an irreconcilable difference between that, and making a sage effective—and safe—for the priesthood.

"You know I'm against the fear-based decisions the priesthood is making now," Learned Muka says. "I advocated to give you space—"

"And you advised me how to weather the storm," I agree, "but not how to break it against me."

Learned Muka sighs and looks at me with concern.

But she won't touch me to anchor me. Not like Tasa did.

"This way is much harder," she tells me. "Be sure."

At that, I let out a humorless laugh. "I'm sure of *nothing*."

"Then get sure fast." Her voice is hard. "Because you're risking more than yourself."

Specifically, I realize, I'm risking her. "You can report that you didn't find me."

"You just told me you don't know what you want. If you decide to come back, what then?"

Then I'd make a liar of her. And if she is forsworn, that would mean death.

Damn it. *Damn* it.

"Here's what we're going to do," Learned Muka says. "You need time to get your head on straight, and I can't stay here and help you. If you want both of us to not die, we give them the dragon."

Now it's my turn to freeze. "*What?*"

"*Think*, Sage Kovan. I tell them I found dragon scales." Learned Muka holds one up—charred; wounded. "It'll redirect attention away from this movement toward controlling sages to fighting dragons. The priesthood will assume you're dead, and you'll be left alone."

Left *with Tasa*, in peace.

For the price of the brethren of the dragon who rescued me from my own people.

"I don't like this," I tell her slowly. "We shouldn't be redirecting persecution toward a different target; we should be stopping it."

"And are you prepared to stand against the entire priesthood?" Learned Muka returns without pause. "All your fellow sages? Is that what you want? You *will* die then, Sage Kovan. Just like the Sage of Wrath did."

Yora isn't dead.

I don't have proof of that, though; only Zan's belief.

Even if the Sage of Wrath isn't technically dead, the distinction is meaningless.

Is that what I want to spend my resolve on? A statement as grand as hers, with even less effect?

Because even I could be overwhelmed by a combined force of priests and sages prepared to fight me.

Would it matter to take a stand, to speak my truth—if I can find it—for no one to hear it?

It's Tasa that cuts through our staring contest, by yanking the water glass out of the Learned's hand.

For the first time, Learned Muka appears to see her.

"How dare you," Tasa tells her. "You do not get to just sacrifice other people for your own convenience."

Learned Muka rolls her eyes. "We're talking about a dragon, girl—"

"*Get out of my house.*"

Now it's my turn to look at Tasa as though I haven't seen her before.

And maybe I haven't.

I've seen her indecisive. I've seen her not believe in herself. I've wanted her to find her resolve.

But right now, she isn't concerned with herself. She's concerned with what is right.

She is *blazing* with it.

Through no help from me.

"Move," Tasa says again in a low, furious voice. "If I have to roll you down the mountain, I will."

In other circumstances, that threat would make me smile.

Now, though—

Now, it feels like even though she's looking at my mentor, the person I learned everything of value from—

Her scorn is for *me*.

"I can't stay anyway," Learned Muka says gruffly, getting to her feet.

As though it's only a sage's working that can sway her, not the choices of a person who has to bake their own bread; as if my magic makes me more of a person.

Learned Muka meets my eyes and says, "This will buy us time. You have until my return to come up with a better idea."

I take her meaning. The priests will debate—once she reports her experience climbing the mountain, no one will be anxious to make the trip, certainly not in the numbers required to hunt a dragon.

But with a suspected location for a hibernating dragon—because they will connect what I was slow to—they won't delay forever.

The woman who raised me doesn't spare even a second glance for Tasa as she leaves, while Tasa holds the door furiously for her and then slams it behind her.

For a moment, we just stare at each other. Braced.

Minutes ago, we were braced for something else entirely.

That seems like a different universe now.

As Tasa whispers furiously, "How *dare* you?"

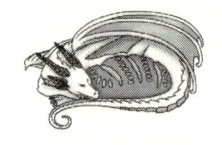

TASA

I can't believe I thought he was different.

I can't believe I let him into my home.

I'm so angry I don't know where to begin, but I know if I wait for him, he'll try to rationalize it, make me feel like I'm overreacting.

People always do.

So when Kovan—*Sage Kovan*—opens his mouth at last, I speak first.

"That dragon saved you," I tell him. "That dragon has done *nothing* wrong—"

"You don't know that—"

"You don't know either! And it doesn't *matter*. You're going to sacrifice a *person*—and don't you dare to try to tell me Zan isn't a person—for your own gain. There is *no* way that is not horrible, *Sage Kovan*."

He flinches.

Good.

And then he says quietly, "I don't know how to make your sanctuary safe again."

Argh. That is so much worse for my righteous fury than trying to justify it to me.

But it's also super not fair to make it *my* fault that Zan is going to die.

Like if I hadn't talked to Zan, if I hadn't make him think he was safe to come back here when I can't actually save anyone, least of all myself and certainly not a dragon, that he wouldn't have risked himself.

I somehow squeeze the words out from my tight throat to ask, "Do you think I'm going to feel safe in a place that requires a person—dragon *or* sage—to be sacrificed?"

Kovan clenches his fists. "I don't know what else you would have me do. Would you rather I die and then they kill Zan anyway?"

Nope, there's the rage again! "Well for starters, you could have said *absolutely not* when that woman suggested it! 'I don't like this'—really? That's all you've got?"

Now he meets my gaze again, and he's beginning to look angry.

Unease coils through me, even though it's what I expected from him.

But then, maybe I'd begun to believe he really was different. That I *could* expect better from this one person.

"Learned Muka was right, Tasa," Kovan's voice comes, low and frustrated. "I *can't* stand up against the full might of the priesthood. Not as I am now, and definitely not here. Do you understand? *I can't do anything.*"

"*Everyone* can do something. Everyone. How dare you give up—and condemn someone to death—before you've even *tried*. You're aware that other people who aren't sages manage to do things every day?"

"Not like this," Kovan snaps.

"Yes, *like this*—"

"Other people who aren't sages cannot wreak the kind of damage I can if I am not perfectly in control and clear in my intention every moment of every day," Kovan overrides me heatedly. "Other people are not walking weapons. You can walk away from your problems and hide in the mountains and no one will come hunting you. You have an endless array of skills that are *not* about being a weapon. It is easy for you to say I can simply try like any other person, but I am *not* any other person. *I am a sage.*"

The heat of my anger drains away, leaving something very hard and brittle in its place.

"Yes," I finally say. "You are a sage, aren't you? I see that now."

The gold in his eyes intensifies, recognizing the insult in my words.

I'm only getting started.

"The real difference between you and me," I continue, "is that no one cares about me, Sage Kovan. Because the *difference* is that you have the ability to control your life and the world around you.

"You think that I'm frivolous, don't you? Flighty, unserious. Everyone does. But *you* have never had to learn how to be funny as a reflex, how to make yourself more palatable, so people would like you despite the problems you bring. Because if they don't like you, they won't be invested in you, but *you*, you are a sage, and you have never had to care about that.

"You have never had to learn how to remake your entire life because how it works depends on someone else. You have never had to look out for yourself because no one else will. You have never had to worry that you had nothing to offer the world—your question is a matter of *how*.

"So if I seem... if I seem *blithe*, Sage Kovan, it is because every day I *choose* to try to be happy, because no one else is in my corner to do it for me. I *choose* to believe that I, and my happiness, matter even when no one else thinks so.

"And I think it is past time you learn how to choose, too, and not make other people bear the consequences for your existence. I thought that was what you wanted. If it isn't—I think you should go back down the mountain, too."

Tears spill out of my eyes despite my best efforts to hold them back. I hate being an angry crier.

I hate how shaky I feel just speaking my truth. How vulnerable to let myself just *be* in front of a man who *doesn't like* the idea of sacrificing a dragon but that's as far as his action will go.

I think I especially hate that I thought maybe this was a person who could actually see me and care about me—he *didn't* think I lacked determination, he covered me with blankets—but at the first sign of adversity there's no substance to him.

To the *sage of resolve.*

And if not him, then... maybe there's no one.

Okay, yes, this is big adversity. Still.

I guess it's better that I learn this now, before I get in any deeper.

Stupid, Tasa, always jumping first—

"You should worry far less than me about having anything to offer," the sage finally says.

For the love of the gods—shit, maybe not love, given who he represents—how is *that* the point he took from this?!

"*You*," Kovan continues, "took pieces of this world no one else saw a use for and built a home."

I wipe my tears in frustration. "Yeah, and it's crooked—"

"It's *art*, Tasa."

"How does that matter, Kov—*Sage* Kovan? People don't choose houses for character, they want to keep the snow out! And I want to *live*."

Kovan nods slowly. "Yes. And you should. And your house is art *and* keeps the snow out. Maybe people should be choosier about where they spend their lives."

I'm not sure what conversation we're having anymore.

"It's easy for you to say that," I whisper. "You, who've never had to choose. Now when you can, when you have to, it's not so simple to be righteous, is it? You're not going to choose the dragon over the priest. And that's a *terrible* decision to have to make, I'm not saying I don't understand. I do.

"Because no one chooses me."

Not all of my teachers over the years, whose various "this just isn't working out" speeches blend together in my mind.

Not my childhood friends, whose invitations gradually stopped coming the more I missed, and the more I broke.

Not my parents, who moved away as soon as I was old enough to start earning by myself, unable to stand a constantly broken home a second longer even if it meant staying with their child.

That's why I'm alone on a mountain, after all. *Hiding from my problems.* More like accepting reality and trying to make the most of it.

A null won't ever be anyone's choice.

I almost miss it when Kovan finally says, "I would."

When I look up, his eyes are fierce again.

And they're meeting my gaze—boldly, firmly. Like he's determined and not ashamed and defensive.

For the first time since the priestess arrived.

And for the first time since she left, my lips smile.

Not my heart, though. And the movement is a bitter one.

"You have only known me for a day," I remind him.

"You are right," Kovan says slowly. "But I have seen enough. You haven't seen enough of *me* to believe me, though—and nor should you, after what I've shown you so far. But I *will* choose you, Tasa. And everything that means."

What in the world *does* that mean?

Oh gods, if he's going to just take on *my* conscience as his moral compass in place of the priesthood's ideals, that is not a responsibility I want.

Maybe that makes me a hypocrite, that I'm not willing to be in charge of his choices either. But that's because they should be *his*.

But also absolutely because I of all people could not be trusted with a sage's power.

I start, "That's not what I meant—"

"Do you have a basket?"

I pause. "What?"

"A basket," Kovan repeats. "A bowl. A bucket. A vessel to hold items, ideally that one could carry—"

"Yes, I know what a basket is, thank you. Why?"

"Because you are right," he says again.

My heart thumps. *He doesn't say things he doesn't mean.*

"Because this is my problem to fix—*my* burden," Kovan says, "not yours."

"And you... need a basket."

"If you don't have one, I will find another—"

"No, that's not—oy." I cross into the kitchen, throw open a few cabinets until I find it, and haul it back to him. "Here."

"Thank you," he says, too seriously.

It is a *basket*.

But maybe—maybe it's also a choice.

And helping someone be able to make it.

When Kovan finally, finally moves—it's toward the front door.

"Are you going to go down the mountain?" I ask softly.

He pauses, turns.

His golden eyes are fierce.

"I'm thinking," he says.

And then he leaves.

CHAPTER 6

KOVAN

Thinking, thinking, thinking.

I can't decide whether I have spent my entire life doing nothing but thinking, or none of my life doing any meaningful thinking.

Possibly both.

Not everything is either-or.

My lack of resolve, though—that stops now.

If I can do nothing else with my life, I will do whatever I can to make Tasa happy.

So a woman as bright as her need never despair like that again.

So she never feels unsafe, unseen, and unvalued in her own home again.

If that means leaving, I will.

But not yet.

No one chooses me, she said, and even as I wanted to gather her hand again in mine and squeeze it tight and let her feel how hard I will try to hold on to her, as I wanted to lash out against everyone who had ever made her feel this way, I felt my resolve surge in me for the first time in weeks.

Choosing Tasa is right.

Even if kissing her is no longer available to one such as me.

If choosing her is a thing no one else can do, or has the will to do, then this *is* the scope for a sage.

It is the scope for a *person*.

Perhaps she is right, that it is not normal for a person to be so committed after a single day.

But I am not a normal person.

I may learn how to bake bread, but that will never change that I am always, always a sage.

A divine vessel.

But perhaps there is a reason that I, specifically, am the bearer of this power, and it is not simply my capacity for resolve.

Determination can be practiced, and I have. But so has Learned Muka.

It galls me to decide that the dragon was correct, after all.

But I am deciding this because doing so means that I *can* be better for Tasa.

I had previously resolved to mitigate the adverse effect of my presence in her life. Now I have simply been made aware that the challenge was even greater than I realized.

But I am the Sage of Resolve, and I am not giving up.

I am doubling down.

That's what I do.

And that, Learned Muka should have known.

So: the immediate problem to address is that I have led the priesthood to Tasa's sanctuary. I cannot undo it, but I can keep the problem from compounding.

The first step is to remove the dragon scales, so they have no evidence of Zan's presence and no trail to follow.

The priests will still try to scale the mountain, but Learned Muka *did* buy me time. And they will struggle like she did.

I will find a way to block them, if I have to climb the mountain myself until I pass the sphere of the Sage of Wrath's influence.

First, I gather every single precious dragon scale sparkling against the earth like flowers, as Yora's presence, *her* choice—and what it must have taken to get there—in Celestial Sanctuary Temple looms large before me.

Here, now, burgeoning, is my most dangerous resolution.

The priests will not have a single scale more from Sanctuary Isle.

Not from Zan, vulnerable in his slumber.

Not from Tasa, alone and unprotected.

And not from me.

Awakening at last.

TASA

Fine, so self-control is not my strength.

I keep peeking out the window to see if Kovan is still here.

Sage Kovan, I try to make myself think.

But it's not sticking.

Because the most powerful magic worker in the empire is just carrying a basket—*my* basket, with dried flowers drooping brittle-ly off the handle, because I haven't looked at that basket in a bit and didn't think to untie them before handing it to a sage—around on his arm like it's the most natural thing in the world as he manually picks up each scale one by one.

At first, Kovan is so focused on his thoughts that he doesn't notice me. And why would he?

Except then he *does*.

It has to be magic, right? I know the Sage of Wrath suppressed magic here, but there's no way Kovan could have known that right at that exact second I was staring at him through the window.

But he looks up.

His golden gaze fixes on mine.

I freeze.

It's like his whole body goes still, utterly focused on me.

And then obviously I panic and duck away.

But after a few minutes of banging around ineffectually in my workshop, I peek again.

Kovan doesn't look this time.

But his lips quirk.

Like he *knows*.

That I'm looking.

That I am panicking about being perceived.

This is somehow worse.

I stomp away to find something else to work on and am irritated all over again when I realize I can actually find what I'm looking for.

How dare he be actually useful when I'm mad at him?

And I *am* mad at him. Kovan messed up with the priest, big time. Maybe I managed to convince him of that, but he still didn't actually apologize.

Then he *left*, without actually leaving, or telling me one way or another what he's going to do so I can't just write him off cleanly yet.

I go to glare at him through the window—

—only to see him tying fresh, lovely wildflowers onto the handle of the basket.

My heart tries to melt in my chest.

I absolutely don't let it.

But this is past enough.

I stalk out of the house, throwing open the front door and putting my hands on my hips.

"What do you think you're doing?" I demand.

The sage looks up.

That golden gaze again. The light catches his eyes, making them look like they're glowing.

All for me.

My breath freezes in my chest as Kovan walks toward me, never blinking.

And then he holds out the dead flowers.

"I wasn't sure if you were saving these on purpose," he says.

Stupid, stupid for my eyes to prick with tears that even after I yelled at him he still assumes by default that my opinions have value, that I think and do things on purpose and not because I'm a giant mess.

Maybe, a treacherous part of me thinks, because *he* thinks.

And is also a much bigger mess than most people know.

"I meant to," I find myself saying. "But they're not worth anything now."

Kovan frowns at me.

Then he sets the dead flowers on top of a veritable fortune in dragon scales.

Like they still matter.

I can't let myself believe in him. Not again.

Even if I wish people would give *me* more chances, this is *different*.

Isn't it?

"What do you plan to do with those?" I ask harshly. "Buy off the priests?"

Kovan's severe expression somehow grows severer, and I resist the urge to shrink away. "No."

I wait.

"That's it?" I finally ask. "Just no?"

He scowls. "I understand why you would ask me that. Learned Muka would praise the idea, and might have thought of it herself if she'd been under less duress. But no, I am not going to give or sell Zan's magic to the priests who would kill him. They cannot have any more of him."

Stupid, treacherous heart.

But I dared the man to try, and he *is*.

The admission makes me angrier, but— "I can't keep them safe here."

He nods. "You will not have to."

"Are *you* keeping them, then? Or hiding them?"

Kovan breathes out. "Since Zan still had power, as do his scales, I thought I might use them to power a barrier, preventing the priests from scaling the mountain at all. But I can't make it work."

Then he meets my eyes again and says in a low voice that strikes my core like a bell, "But I will make something work."

Damn it.

Damn it.

It would be so much easier to just write him off.

To not risk letting him be able to hurt me again.

But that's not who I want to be, is it?

That's why I let him in at all.

That's why I dared talk back to a sage.

I'm not going to let other people's fear close me off to the magic of this world.

I pick up one of the tiny, shimmering white scales. On a dragon, all the scales together look like armor. Alone like this, they look like I could crush them between my fingers.

Wryly, I realize there's an obvious metaphor here. Thanks, universe, I get it. Blargh.

"You should try farther away from the temple," I tell Kovan.

At the same time he says to me, "You're not nullifying the magic of the scales."

I blink at him. "What?"

"I can still sense magic," Kovan explains. "It's how I am locating all the scales. Your magic *doesn't affect them*."

My hand holding the dragon scale shakes.

Which is stupid. A sage just told me I *wasn't* breaking them.

But I break *everything*.

So I drop the scale back into the basket, with the dead flowers and the beautiful scales I shouldn't risk touching, and it feels like my heart goes with it.

Because it would be too much to have this and then find out later I could break it after all.

"I don't have magic," I say numbly, reflexively. "I have the opposite of magic. I'm like a magic void."

Kovan steps in close enough that he can cup my face in his free hand.

I stare, my heart hammering.

"You could not affect magic without magic of your own," he says fiercely. "You may be the most powerful being on Sanctuary Isle."

"Okay, *that* is ridiculous."

More powerful than him, or the Sage of Wrath, the strongest magic workers in the empire?

More powerful than Zan, an actual dragon?

"It isn't," Kovan says. But he drops his hand.

Not letting it go, I think. But deciding I'm not ready to hear what he has to say.

That hurts, way more than I expected.

But then he says, "Will you take me to Crystal Hollow? Since you've said magic is more variable at the base of the mountain, perhaps I can combine the dragon scales with the wards there."

And I realize that maybe I'm not ready after all.

Not ready for him to see what's become of our village, how little I've actually managed when he seems to think the world of me.

Not ready for him to see what everyone else thinks of me, to see him turn away from me.

But I always knew that was coming, didn't I?

I *won't* decide for him.

I *won't* let fear make me too cowardly to reach for magic in the world.

But I still know it's better to get burned by banked embers than by a roaring flame; better to know sooner than later if he, like everyone else, can't cope with all of me.

Even if part of me knows that it's already far too late to avoid crumbling to ashes in his wake.

"Good idea," I say lightly. "Let's try."

CHAPTER 7

TASA

Our hike down the mountain starts silently.

It's an itchy kind of silence, at least for me.

The urge to just pretend everything is okay, to smooth over the awkwardness, is *really* strong. It's a defense mechanism for me.

But everything *isn't* okay.

And at least while I'm on this mountain, I get to have boundaries.

My chest tightens, and not with exertion.

Because of course, we're currently leaving the place where I get to hold space for myself.

I count it as a small victory that it's the sage and not me who finally breaks the silence.

But what he says is, "I understand that it is through my own actions that you cannot trust me now. Until I can prove myself to you, is there anything I can do—in addition to baking bread—to make being around me easier for you?"

My brain full-on freezes.

No one *ever* tries to make things easier for *me*. That's always my job.

But my body keeps moving, and that basic disconnect between the attempt to freeze and not freeze causes me to trip over a big branch that's fallen in the path.

I flail for a second and hear Kovan sharply say, "*Brace.*"

But there's nothing to brace *on*, and I hear him swear as I fall, about to land on my face—

And then Kovan catches me.

Not only does he catch me, he scoops me up in his arms.

Why in the world does a sage have the muscles to hold me so easily? Which god hates me?

(Resolve, obviously.)

I lick my lips and manage to say, "Thank you."

Yeah, it's a little breathy. Cut me some slack, I'm only mortal.

But so is even a sage, and Kovan's eyes track the movement, his gaze fixing on my lips for a moment.

He swallows.

Meets my gaze.

There's a moment where I am absolutely sure he's about to kiss me, for real this time—

And then his golden gaze shutters.

He takes a deep breath—actually cringes—and then gently sets me down on my own feet, looking away.

It's stupid to be so disappointed when *I am still mad at him.*

But I *am* hurt, and I lash out, "My apologies to the mighty sage for troubling you with my scent when I didn't ask you to save me."

Kovan's gaze flies back to mine. "I don't dislike your scent, Tasa. Quite the opposite."

...Oh.

My cheeks warm.

Well, shit. He's trying to be careful with my boundaries *because* he knows I'm mad at him. Even if I might kind of want him to just kiss me and pretend everything is fine between us so I don't have to think about it, that's not actually fair to him *or* me.

"And *I* apologize," Kovan says, "for being so dependent on magic that I nearly failed to save you from the fall that I distracted you into at all."

Oh, *that's* what he meant by "brace." He tried to catch me with magic first, falling back on a lifetime of training... that didn't help him.

"You were still fast enough," I tell him softly.

Kovan takes a breath and lets it out. "No." His gaze meets mine fiercely. "Demonstrably I have not been. But I *will* become fast enough to keep up with you, Tasa."

We're not talking about the fall anymore.

At least, not mine.

Maybe I'm being too harsh with him. Being unwilling to stand up for Zan unequivocally *is* bad, but I am also expecting him to undo the habits of a lifetime in days.

Kovan has never had to go against the priesthood before. He's never had the option to stand up for what he believes in before, not to mention even decide for himself what that is.

But being angry with him is so much safer than the alternative.

And that thought, ultimately, is what makes me let it go.

"When someone says 'thank you'," I say, "the appropriate response is 'you're welcome'. Not cringing and backing away. If you're looking for ways to make your presence easier on people around you."

Kovan pinches the bridge of his nose, which makes *me* cringe. I know what follows that put-upon expression—

"I suppose kissing you until neither of us can breathe isn't an appropriate response either," he says wryly.

—aaand it's absolutely not that.

The faint amusement on his face vanishes when he sees that I've frozen again.

"My sincerest apologies, that was—"

Somehow what emerges from my mouth to interrupt him is: "It might do as a substitute, in certain circumstances."

Now Kovan freezes.

"Like, maybe not while I'm in the middle of tending a fire, right?" I babble. "Because then I'd get distracted and burn the house down—"

His mouth touches mine.

Everything else in the world goes still for me.

It's like I can distill this moment: birds chirp in the trees, a background of song; the sun shines down on us, like for once *I* am in the spotlight; a gentle breeze flutters around me, touching me, anchoring me in the moment so I can believe it's real.

Our eyes are both wide open.

I see the flicker of insecurity in his gaze as neither of us move. So before he can, I do:

Stepping closer to him.

Moving my lips against his.

That insecurity turns to something like blank shock, and I have a moment to feel a surge of confidence that *I* did that, to a *sage*, before it occurs to me that maybe he didn't actually *like* it—

And then his arms wrap around me and he closes his eyes, as if all he wants is to savor the feeling of me against him, and my own eyes finally flutter shut with his because that's what I want, too.

The moment is already so perfect, but I am who I am and I can't help pushing. My tongue meets his lips, and he gasps—

And then draws away.

Before I can rear back, Kovan's arms tighten around me and he rests his forehead against mine, breathing hard.

I swallow. I need to stop leaping to conclusions with him; need to stop reacting to him as though he's of a piece with other people. He *has* already proven that he's not. In so many ways, he's not, and not because he's a sage.

This is *my* habit to break.

"Too fast?" I whisper.

His lips curve in a smile that makes me want to melt into him.

"I don't deserve the joy of you as I am now," Kovan says.

That's... not what I expected. "What about what I deserve?"

Gently, he tucks a lock of my hair behind my ear. "Before I take advantage of your good nature and distract you from my failures, at the very least you deserve an apology.

"I *am* sorry. For making you less safe in your home. For making you feel uncertain with me. *You are welcome*, Tasa. Ask whatever you will of me."

Crying is not an appropriate response to kissing, but I'm struggling to hold it back as I tighten my hold on him.

You are welcome. I so want to believe in that.

I don't, quite. I believe he means it now; I am less certain he'll mean it in another hour or two once we've been to the village.

But what I really want from him is: "Will you apologize for making me wonder whether you're going to leave me or not?"

My voice comes out more strained than I'd prefer, because I'm trying to keep it together, but I really want to shrivel up and pretend I didn't just ask for something for myself that reveals so much.

Kovan looks dumbfounded for a moment, like once again I've verbally bopped him on the nose.

Then he tightens his arms around me, squeezing me to his chest as he hugs me.

"Living with you is an endlessly humbling experience," he says. "My failures are never what I think they are. I am sorry most of all for making you feel insecure about *me*, Tasa, and how I think of you. I don't want to leave you. I don't know how I can stay. I don't know how I can make your life better, but I am trying, and I will keep trying, and as long as I am not making it worse for you, I want to stay with you."

Damn him. Now I am crying.

I bury my face in his shirt. "This is stupid," I mutter. "It's been like two days."

Yes, I hyper-fixate, but I shouldn't be this attached.

But Kovan doesn't agree. He just holds me.

And he says, "Powerful magic works fast."

I reject the instinctual, bitter thought that there can never be magic for me of all people.

Because one thing I can trust him to be an expert on is magic.

And I do want to believe in it for me. For us.

I lift my head to meet his gaze again.

Kovan swears under his breath when he sees my tears, which makes me smile a little.

"So now what?" I ask.

"Now—"

He kisses me again.

This time it's languid, and dizzying, and I do let myself melt into him.

Let someone hold me up, for once.

When we finally pull apart, it isn't far; and both of us are breathing hard.

"Now," Kovan says in a hoarse voice, then clears his throat. "I know you're worried about taking me to Crystal Hollow."

I immediately tense in his arms, and he nods.

"I can go by myself, if that would be easier—"

"No." I let my arms drop. "No, I think this matters."

Better for him to see.

Better for me to know.

Kovan nods again. "I know you can't believe me yet. But no one can make me doubt you."

He's right; I don't believe that.

Maybe this is a sage thing, or a resolve thing, that he just assumes he'll be unaffected by me the way everyone else is.

He is different.

But no one has ever been that different.

Kovan takes my hand; squeezes it. "Help me try?" he asks softly. "And then we'll go home."

My heart clenches.

It's too late for me already.

So I squeeze his hand once before letting go and just say, "Let's go."

It's too bad that he managed to reassure me about where I stand with him just in time to throw that shaky foundation against a mountain.

It always cracks.

KOVAN

THE REST OF OUR hike down the mountain is almost unbearably sweet.

Tasa knows *everything* about what is on this mountain. She can identify everything from slugs to moss and enthusiastically tell me their histories and likes and dislikes and hopes and fears, as if they have been her friends when no one else would.

What makes it unbearable is that she has been safer to share herself with the moss than with the people in her life.

What makes it unbearable is that I know she is still doubting me.

What makes it unbearable is that I haven't proven yet that I will be able to keep myself in her life, when I want this hike to be one of many for us.

So when we reach the end of it I want to both hold her to me and kiss her sweet lips again and never leave the mountain, and I want to charge ahead and raze this village that's made her doubt herself to the ground.

But the village is not the only problem; I am.

So I don't reach for Tasa when she squares her shoulders, pastes on a bright, *false* smile, and leads the way, putting space between us. I let her lead; I let her take care of herself the way she knows how.

But I do close the distance.

Because right now, I *am* with her.

Tasa glances at me; swallows; continues on.

(She, too, has practiced resolve.)

And Crystal Hollow unfolds before us.

I can see vestiges of what beauty it must have been before; sides of buildings that are still picturesque, a motley of stones that are now a kind of path, all nestled in the forested landscape.

But the village looks like it exploded.

I am looking at a village in pieces, reassembled imperfectly, while destruction still fills the streets.

Tasa weaves through walls fallen at diagonals covering the paths, sliding over and ducking through and casually picking up chunks—bits of siding and door knobs and iron works—to put into her pack.

She doesn't even notice when I take some pieces out of her hands to drop them into my pack instead.

Tasa takes her time at this, and I think she is simply distracted by the copious interesting detritus around until we come far enough that we begin to hear voices.

Tasa doesn't slow further.

But I can *see* the tension growing in her shoulders.

Long before an elderly woman spots her and snaps, "Tasa! Where have you been? My kitchen sink still doesn't work!"

Tasa approaches and stops a few feet short.

The elderly woman still takes a step back, glaring.

The *audacity*—

"Sorry about that!" Tasa says. "I had something unexpected come up—"

The woman snorts derisively.

"—but I'm here now. Is your bathroom sink still working?"

"Yes, you didn't break that one, but I can't be hauling my vegetables back and forth all the time. You know how my knees get. Come now, before you *forget* again, lazy girl."

"I'm afraid I am the unexpected occurrence that came up," I tell the woman in an even tone before I can punch her in the face with my actual fist like a barbarian. "Tasa has been ensuring I didn't die without supplies while looking into the magical situation here. My apologies to your knees."

The old woman narrows her eyes at me. "Don't sass me, young man. If you're giving her an excuse to flake out on the one job she can do—"

Tasa interrupts, "I'll be there as soon as I can, I promise, but I got word of some sparking magic that I have to see to first."

She can lie, at least. I appreciate the utility now in a way I never have before.

Tasa continues, "You know your next-door neighbor will bring you a casserole if your knees need a break."

"*I* can cook for my own self, thank you," the woman says coldly before stalking off.

I look at Tasa. "Am I correct to assume you're the reason any of them have functioning water in their homes right now at all?"

She looks back, and I hate the weariness in her gaze. "She doesn't want to be dependent on anyone, certainly not me, and I don't blame her for that. She's known me a lot longer than you have, Kovan. You're not going to convince anyone I'm some kind of savior, because I'm not. I've made their lives harder my whole life."

I open my mouth, but she cuts me off and says, "Stop trying to tell me otherwise and *listen*."

That draws me up short.

And when she continues walking without saying anything more, I realize what she means.

I've spent my whole life listening to the priesthood first and foremost, not to the people, unfiltered.

So now I do.

I watch every person we pass demand things from Tasa—finding parts for a stove, checking on a malfunctioning toilet, moving a piece of debris for them, which I even help with, to alarmed expressions that *I*, a stranger, should not risk myself.

All of this from a 'safe' distance.

They want her labor, but not her.

Meanwhile Tasa responds to *everyone* cheerfully, by name, without complaint and only rarely with redirection. She gives all of herself and respects *their* boundaries even if it breaks her heart, without enforcing any of her own.

Except that she doesn't let them see her hurt.

She let me.

It's sinking in how rare that must be for her.

Just as rare as a sage trying to find himself anew.

I stay close to Tasa the whole time, daring anyone willing to meet my gaze to see me standing next to her. Watching every person meet my gaze with abject confusion or even horror.

Only one man appears to look away in guilt.

At last Tasa comes to a stop in a quiet section where we're alone, and it's immediately apparent why: she's somehow made a pile here of detritus from Crystal Hollow.

"Welcome to my junk heap!" Tasa announces in that same false, cheerful voice, and I can't take it anymore.

"Don't perform here, Tasa," I say quietly. "Not for me."

She pauses, and her smile falls away.

"If we go a little farther, I know where one of the closest wards is," Tasa says instead. "You can test—"

"It's not a *junk heap*," I say furiously, stepping toward her. "And I don't care about the wards."

She blinks quickly. "Wait. You're upset for *me*?"

Gods, how does she even have to ask that—

But I know, don't I? I just watched.

I just glimpsed exactly why she lives alone on a mountain.

Where I had the gall to tell her she was hiding from her problems.

I couldn't have been more wrong.

She was finally establishing a godsdamned boundary.

And maybe—maybe that's what I've done too, fleeing to a mountain.

"Do you ever say no?" I ask her quietly. "Do you feel like you can?"

She blinks but answers, "Not if I can help it? I mean, what else am I supposed to do? I can finally help them for once."

"For *once*? What *else*? You're the reason they're all alive right now, and they treat you like—"

"Whoa, okay, I feel like we just had two very different experiences—"

"*Clearly.*"

"—but cut them some slack, okay? Their entire way of life just collapsed, and *they* didn't choose it."

"So did yours, and you're restoring theirs and they won't even come *near* you—"

"I mean as far as they know I could be making it worse, right? Most people can't sense magic like you can." I clench my jaw so hard I fear my teeth will crack, and Tasa continues, "And I am also benefitting from the destruction of their lives, so I can forgive them for being a little salty about it, you know? They have to depend on the resident fuck-up that they know they can't trust just to survive."

I carefully take a breath and unclench my jaw.

It still takes me a moment before I can finally say, "I think you may not understand precisely how angry every word you just said makes me."

She blinks again, like my perspective is completely inexplicable to her, which does nothing to tamp down my fury. "Yeah, I'm... getting that impression? So um." Tasa runs her hands through her hair. "Do you want to see the ward, or—"

"No."

"No? I thought you wanted to help."

I listened.

I watched.

Now I need to make a decision.

Now I need to go to work.

What Tasa needs—what these people need—is not, I think, a shield, like I had been planning.

What Tasa wants is a place where she can feel safe.

What she needs is the freedom to grow.

One big work will not change the villagers' attitudes toward Tasa; it might even worsen them, because then they won't feel that she's useful at all. Their opinions of her did not originate with the Quieting, and they won't vanish if it's removed.

In the same way that making Tasa believe in me will take many acts, it will take time to make them see her.

I don't think they deserve to, but: it will make Tasa happier.

So.

"Can you find something in this collection that needed magic to function?"

Tasa huffs. "Collection, like it's curated. Don't pretend I'm some kind of savior, Kovan."

"I said what I meant. You literally collected all these pieces here."

"Sure, but not with like, grand intent—"

"Do you not discover what you can do with them once you have them in one place? If this is how your art works, to flourish from a mass of chaos you can build something new from, then that is your process. I don't care what it looks like, and neither should anyone else, and if they do I will punch them."

Tasa startles. "You will not."

"I'm considering it," I growl. My magic might not be effective, after all, and I wouldn't want to miss.

"Kovan. Look, it's not art—"

"I disagree, and since I have lived in a cottage that you built, you will not convince me otherwise. But to my question, Tasa—can you find a piece with failed magic?"

"Oh, sure, what *doesn't* have failed magic," she mutters.

But she stops arguing with me, so I will take it, even aware that she also did not agree.

She's staring a little lost at the junk heap, though, and I quickly realize my error. I haven't known Tasa long, but I have worked with other people who benefitted from the kind of focus magic that no one can provide her with. I've left her with too open-ended a request, given that I have a specific purpose in mind; she'll likely feel more confident if I narrow the scope to a specific task.

Well, we're *not* helping the elderly woman first who took her own insecurity out on someone she considered a safe target. Imagining how often Tasa, who tries harder than anyone I've met, has been called *lazy* because of how her mind works—

Deep breaths.

I cast back to the person who at least had the awareness to realize that how the villagers are treating Tasa is shameful, and what he asked for.

"What about the man who needed help with his stove?"

"Oh, Noten?" Her whole being lights up, and it makes me ache.

Making her happy is *so* simple after all—giving her the chance to help someone with what she *can* do—and yet—

"Yeah, what he was saying makes it sound like he just needs a new fire lighter—most stoves come with a little spell that stabilizes it. Pretty sure I have a dead one in here somewhere. Give me a few minutes, it's a small piece and I don't know how to describe what it looks like."

"Take your time."

I'll need that time to figure out my part.

I begin a meditative kata, sorting out the threads with my movement.

Not a holding pattern, but weaving different threads.

What I was trying before was a shield; setting myself in opposition to the Sage of Wrath's power.

But while Crystal Hollow is, in its way, vulnerable, it is not like Zan.

The village doesn't need to be defended, not in its current form. It needs to change.

Knowingly or not, Yora started that work here.

But she didn't finish it, because wrath is about waves, and she set off only one—an incomparably vast one, to be sure, but a single wave nonetheless.

My movements slow with deliberation; less sharpness; no breaks.

Resolve is different.

Resolve is steady.

Resolve is continual.

Resolve is putting in time even when it feels unsatisfying in the moment, because it's not about the moment.

It's about Tasa.

Tasa, who needs safety she can trust. Who needs to feel less pressure to make other people happy at her own expense. Who needs them to appreciate her when they're not dependent on her.

An idea takes root, and I spin with it.

This will take time.

But I can feel aching wisps of magic here on the Quiet Side, and I am powerful enough in my own right to make something of what is here for me.

When I open my eyes, Tasa is watching me wide-eyed, bathed in the soft golden glow of my magic.

I hold a hand out to her, and she drops the tiny instrument into it.

So small, to make a difference.

But it's a start.

Seeds start small, too.

And then they grow.

I slip a tiny dragon scale inside its inner workings.

"Stabilize," I pronounce in a low voice made rich and resonant with the power I channel.

The device flares bright gold, with veins of sparkling white mixed in.

Sage and dragon magic, working together. Not a sight I ever thought to see.

What else have I never imagined?

When the glow fades, I hand it back to Tasa. "Can you seal it so the dragon scale inside can't be seen?"

"Hm? Oh yeah, sure. I can do that when I install it."

She's staring at me like she's seeing me for the first time.

In a way she is; being sage is a part of me, and I imagine the glowing makes it visibly real in a way it previously wasn't to her.

But I have never been a sage like this before.

And I find that it matters to me that this one person sees me as more than a divine vessel.

It's greedy. I've already been chosen by a god.

But I want to be chosen by her.

"You can fix us," Tasa whispers.

I shake my head sharply. "There's nothing to fix. Nothing is broken."

"Actually quite a lot is literally broken—"

"*Tasa.*"

"Yes, okay, this isn't broken exactly, its magic just doesn't work—"

I grip her shoulders. "You're not broken. All of this is the pieces for a new beginning. I can merely strengthen what is already here. *You* are the one who builds."

She blinks.

And a smile spreads across her face, like dawn breaking across the sky.

"And now I won't have to worry that the roof will fall down!" Tasa exclaims. "No no I get it, I still have to pay attention to physics, but—"

"You can build more houses," I say intently. "You can build *whatever you want*. And each will be different, because you'll always be working with different pieces, different needs—"

"And I won't get bored," Tasa whispers. "But—"

I place a finger on her lips. "No buts. This will work. For you, and for Crystal Hollow. My word as a sage."

Tasa was right. I can start with something small that matters and build up.

Now I have to convince her that she already matters.

CHAPTER 8

KOVAN

Tasa practically bounds up to Noten to tell him she can fix his stove—abruptly freezing several steps away but continuing to chatter cheerfully—and my chest squeezes to see it.

I love seeing her happy, and she is effusive with it. She is *so* easily fulfilled by being able to help people with her work.

That she has been so miserable here is damning.

Noten tells her to go right in, as his husband Ichike—feminine name but masculine pronouns, I make a mental note—is there watching his sister's children.

Tasa brightens further at the prospect of seeing the children that Noten wryly calls "the terrors," which makes me freeze long enough that I don't protest when she tells me she'll stop by the awful old woman's house and meet me there.

Sages never partner. We never have children. The temple doesn't want to risk our distraction with such emotional attachments.

So I've never considered whether I would want children, because I never had the option.

But if I don't return to the temple—if I stay with Tasa, and if *she* would want, with me—

Too much; too fast. That's a consideration for after I have made Tasa's world safe for her.

But it's somewhat startling to realize that I am excited to consider the prospect.

Excited by what the world might offer *me*, rather than the other way around.

By the time I've returned to the present moment, Tasa is off, and Noten is watching me warily.

He's recognized me as a danger. True, certainly, though I wonder whom he thinks I'm a danger *to*.

I break the silence, crossing to him. "Your stove will not malfunction again."

Noten's eyes narrow. "You seem awfully sure."

"I am."

Wonder of wonders, given that I have tried a magical working like no one has before under unprecedented circumstances.

But I do not say things I don't mean.

"I asked Ichike to put together some fresh fruit for her," Noten says carefully. "I think it's been a while since anyone's given her that, since no one is willing to let food to go to waste now. But if you're staying with her, perhaps you can remind her of it?"

Anger surges again. That people know Tasa enough to anticipate her habits but not to let her make her own choices. That this man has noticed the problem but not done anything to address it.

Tasa asked me to cut them slack. Their lives have been destroyed.

But in this case, I don't believe heeding her will ultimately make her happy, so I am not going to.

Am I just as bad as everyone else? Not respecting her decisions?

But no: Tasa doesn't get to decide my choices any more than these people should decide hers.

I did ask what I could do for her. But specifically I wanted to decrease my burden on her, and it is also not Tasa's responsibility to decide that for me.

I do not need my decisions made for me any more than Tasa does, and she—and Zan—is the one who called me to account on that. If I want to help, it is on *me* decide what I can and will offer, not her.

"I imagine that Tasa will appreciate your consideration," I reply, making it abundantly clear with my tone that I do not. "But she is not a child. She is doing work, not charity. A functional stove in your circumstances is worth more than food, and you know it.

"So when your stove continues to function, the next time we come through, you will talk to her close by, not like she has a disease. And you will include coin in her payment, so *she* can choose for herself. Do we understand each other?"

Noten has gone still.

I don't know the monetary value of what Tasa has offered.

THE QUIET SIDE

But I know the emotional value of what this would mean to receive.

After a long, considering moment, like Noten is worried any movement will attract the attention of a dragon, he nods slowly.

One seed planted.

Now to rip out a weed that Tasa insists on watering.

Tasa is already hard at work on the old woman's home when I arrive—or so I assume from the banging I hear outside—and as I suspected, the elder is proffering a steady stream of gripes at her.

I knock.

By the time the old woman throws open the door with a glare, I say, with no pretense at pleasantry and no hesitation, "You will not insult Tasa again."

Her eyes narrow at me. "Or what?"

The banging inside is loud enough that I have no fear that Tasa can hear us. "Oh? Must there be threat of reprisal for you to behave with basic courtesy?"

She snorts. "This, coming from the big man on my doorstep who offers no greeting after making an old woman get to her feet? Watch your tongue."

"No," I say.

She blinks at me.

"*You* are dependent on Tasa's charity," I say.

"How dare—"

"Did you plan to pay her, then?"

She glares. "That child—"

"Woman," I correct in a low, dangerous tone.

"—is a menace, and we have been cleaning up her messes her entire life. You know nothing. The least she can do—"

"—is nothing. She could simply leave. Tasa did not break your house. She is fixing it. Everyone else in this village is paid for their work. What are you paying her, except insults?"

"That's what this is?" She demands. "You're extorting me? An old woman whose house has been destroyed?"

"I am informing you of new terms," I tell her coldly. "If you cannot pay in coin, then you will, at a minimum, no longer pay only insults. Or, since you think so little of her, I will make sure she is distracted any time she learns of your needs."

She snorts. "So blackmail then, not extortion."

"If you need to be blackmailed into not treating people poorly," I say, "I can take on that burden for her. So? Will you pay in courtesy, or material wealth?"

I expect her to rail at me.

I am not at all prepared for her to stomp away, leaving the door open behind her.

Keeping my expression even, as if I am very confident about what is happening, I cautiously follow her in.

When I arrive in the kitchen, she slams a crock of butter in front of me and a loaf of bread with a haughty look of challenge.

Like we are in a negotiation.

I push the bread back and inform her, "I will be baking Tasa's bread."

She holds my gaze for a long moment.

Nods sharply.

"Make sure she brings my dish back," she says.

And then storms out of the room without another word.

People are a wonder.

After all this time, and me a sage, I understand them so very little.

Tasa's head pokes up from under the kitchen sink. "What was—Kovan? She let you in? Oh my goodness, is that her *butter*?"

Her gasp is one of wonder and sheer delight.

It is so *easy* to make Tasa happy that even I can manage it.

I am angry all over again that no one else has tried.

She dared me to try.

To start, and to keep going from there.

And I will.

For her, I can do this.

Tasa's head whips around the room in shock, looking for the old woman, before returning to me. "What did you do?!"

The fierceness of my resolve has set me to glowing again.

But I answer the important part of her question.

"I planted a seed."

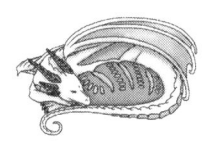

TASA

I'm beginning to feel like I've finally glimpsed the sage inside Kovan.

But, bafflingly, not in a bad way?

At some point, in between me yelling at him and kissing him and chattering about moss at him, and him visiting Crystal

Hollow and seeing what things are like there and glowing at me, Kovan settled into himself.

I'd thought, when we arrived in Crystal Hollow, that I was throwing our shaky foundation against a mountain and bracing for it to crack.

I had it wrong.

Until now I've seen him at his worst, and I still wanted him.

But at his best, he *is* the mountain.

Foundations don't crack with him; he strengthens them by his very being.

That's what it means to be the sage of resolve.

And I'm beginning to feel like what he's resolved is to make me, personally, swoon at his feet.

I honestly can't tell if this is on purpose or just what Kovan's like for everyone? It seems like it couldn't possibly be just for me?

But as soon as we get back to the cottage, he takes the crock from his pack and butters me a piece of the bread that he baked for me.

Then while I chop some vegetables for sandwiches, because Kovan still doesn't know how to put together a meal, it's like he's constantly *there* without me having to think about it.

A steady presence.

Yet somehow he's also everywhere?

Kovan finds a basket for the amazing fruit Noten gifted me with. He puts a glass of water right into my hand and waits until I take a sip and then discover I was parched and down the whole glass. He updates his accounting of our food options. He washes my bread plate. He unpacks my new loot into the workshop.

If *I* were trying to do all these things, I'd lose track of my plan between one task and the next. I'd look like I was fluttering, the wind blowing me around, and yet there's a weight to Kovan; a presence.

An anchor.

As soon as Kovan confirms that I'm done eating, he whisks my plate away to wash the way I taught him and I finally burst out, "Okay *what* is going on here?"

He glances back over his shoulder at me with eyebrows arched and hands deep in soapy water and why does that look sexy? How?

"Could you be more specific?" Kovan asks.

I gesture wildly around. "This. You. You don't have to do all this."

Good work, Tasa, very clear.

"Ah." He carefully puts the dishes away; towels his hands dry slowly.

I will absolutely not be jealous of a towel.

"You are referring, then," Kovan says, "to someone actually trying to take care of *you*, for a change?"

My heart thumps.

Shit. That *is* what I mean, isn't it?

"I don't want to be a burden to *you* any more than you want to be one to me," I manage softly. "I didn't mean to obligate you into anything. You have your own problems—"

Kovan turns to face me, golden eyes glowing, leaning all his lithe strength back against my kitchen counter like he is trying not to be intimidating and instead just managing to be the sexiest person alive.

Uh oh.

"You haven't forced me to do anything except decide what I want," he says, still in that very steady, controlled tone. "And I *want* to do this, Tasa."

"Dishes? No one wants to do dishes." Surely?

"*Take care of you.* And that no one has wanted to do that before is a symptom of a deeper imbalance than what Yora's detonation revealed."

What? "It's not some cosmic problem, it's just because no one actually likes me that much," I say, reasonably.

And get a very unreasonable darkening of his expression in response.

"That," Kovan growls, "is very incorrect."

"That there's a big issue in Crystal Hollow—oh." I break off faintly, swallowing hard as he advances on me deliberately. "You—you meant the other thing, didn't you."

Kovan's in front of me now, and I want to melt into a puddle on the floor in embarrassment but I'm rooted to the spot, staring up into his golden gaze as my face—and maybe somewhere else—heats from the fierceness of his regard.

Maybe now I am finally beginning to understand what a sufficiently motivated sage of resolve is capable of—

All thought vanishes when his mouth crashes into mine.

Our kiss in the forest was sweet.

This one, though—

This one is a force.

Like he can say through lips alone, *Believe how much I want you.*

As his arms come around me to hold me up under the onslaught of more feelings than I can stand, I admit this is very persuasive, even if I still can't quite believe that this is somehow happening. Not in *my* life.

But it is beyond me to stop him. To try to convince him that no, really, he doesn't like me, he's just in a midlife crisis and I happened to be here and he'll surely get fed up with me, just give it time—

As though he can feel my doubts, though, Kovan breaks off our kiss as I strain toward him, embarrassing myself.

But he doesn't draw away. He kisses me again, and again, softer now, as his arms tighten around me.

And when he finally pulls away again it is only to murmur, "I more than simply like you, Tasa," Kovan says. "Allow me to show you how much."

Oh gods.

He's going to destroy me. I'm already practically in love with him, and he's going to ruin me for anyone else—

"Tasa." He kisses me again. "Yes?"

There's only one answer I have it in me to give. "Yes," I whisper.

Pressed close to him like this, I *feel* him shudder with my verbal consent.

And despite it all, that makes me feel a little more powerful.

Then Kovan scoops me up in his arms like carrying me is absolutely trivial and stalks toward the bedroom.

"How are you this strong when you spend your days doing magic?!" I demand.

Kovan huffs his amusement as he settles onto my bed with me in his lap. "Sages train every day. Our forms are physical, because the work we do is in the physical world."

Then he smirks at me and says, "Let me show you what I can do."

Oh gods, like I needed to be *more* impressed—

But Kovan picks me up and maneuvers me so I'm straddling him, and I gasp at the feel of his length against me, already half-hard.

I rock against him, reflexively, and his smirk drops off with a groan of satisfaction.

"Are we really doing this?" I whisper.

This time, for once, I think we're having the same conversation, because Kovan just takes my face in his hands and says, "Yes. For as long as you want me, yes."

His consent, this time.

And it makes me just bold enough to whisper, "Then touch me?"

The gold of his eyes actually flashes, I definitely did not make that up, and then his mouth is on mine again.

But his hands—his hands *move*.

One arm circles behind me, holding me against him.

The other hand covers my breast.

Just that, one bold, claiming touch, and I arch like he's jolted me with lightning.

No one has ever wanted to claim me before.

And the command Kovan has over my body—oh, he is claiming.

He kneads my breast through my shirt slowly—the full weight of it in his large hand already has me squirming, but then he slowly circles my nipple and I still against him, my whole attention focused on that warm point of contact between us.

Then his mouth pulls away from mine, and before I can object he's pressed a kiss to my breast through my clothes.

Every thought in my head whites out in an instant.

And in the next, I am scrambling out of my shirt, because if that's what it feels like with my clothes on, just imagine—nope, on second thought, pretty sure my imagination is not good enough—

Kovan, much more deliberately, pulls his own shirt over his head and I can't help but breathe, "Oh gods."

With his dark hair mussed and the lines of his jaw stark like they are going to shatter, and then his chest like he is carved from fucking alabaster, *how* is he real—

But then I manage to draw my gaze up to his golden eyes, which are devouring the sight of *me*.

And once again, I'm anchored in him.

And bold.

Not quite bold enough to just take off all my clothes at once; maybe this will be as far as he wants to go today.

But bold enough to draw his head toward my naked breast.

Kovan doesn't fight me.

Honestly, that's putting it kind of mildly, because one second I'm making, you know, like, a nonverbal suggestion, and the next he has his mouth on me like he's been dreaming about tasting me, with one hand on my other breast and the other holding me to him like he won't *let* me go and my head falls back, gasping with all the sensation.

I'm pretty sure sages are fucking celibate, but to be the focus of all his attention, and deliberation, and care—

I have never had *anyone* take me apart so quickly. So *thoroughly*.

But no: it's like with every touch, he's putting me back together.

And I can't help but touch him, too, every perfect inch of his skin, and every stroke increases the fire between us until he is hard and I am writhing against him and finally, *finally*, one hand draws down to the juncture of my thighs.

And with it, the entirety of my focus.

I open my eyes to see him looking at me, and if I thought his gaze was fierce before it is *nothing* to what it looks like now.

His voice is low and half-growl as he still asks, "Yes?"

Does he really think I'm going to say no here?

Wait, actually— "Can you remind me to drink some cycle tea later?"

Kovan frowns. "Yes. What does that mean?"

"I can't use magic to help with cramps, but I studied for a while with a woman who taught me how to suppress my monthly cycle with various plants—we foraged some today," I explain. "Obviously I didn't work for her long-term because, you know, paying consistent attention enough to not poison someone accidentally, not going to work for me, but I can still brew that. In all the drama today I forgot to take today's dose though."

Kovan swallows. "You would trust me with this?" he asks roughly. Like *he* can't believe it.

And that actually makes me feel surer about my snap decision, that he does appreciate the momentousness.

Because if he forgot, or didn't care enough about the consequences or what I actually want, this would be a big risk for me.

But it's him, so it's not.

I think he needs the words from me as much as I do from him, though, so I say softly, "Yes."

And this time *I* kiss *him*.

Kovan kisses me desperately, like a drowning man who has discovered air, and it completely defies understanding to me that no one has ever bothered to look at him and see him as a person and not just a sage, to touch him and not just his power, that a person as messy as me can somehow do this to him.

But I can.

Whether I understand or not, I'm not blind.

And since I can, I'm going to do more.

The man has already blown my mind. Surely it's my turn.

So I tear myself away from him and quickly slide off of his lap. Kovan reflexively reaches for me—

—but freezes when I drop my pants and step out of them.

His eyes glow.

I smile. "Your turn."

The sage can move *fast* when motivated. I don't even blink but somehow his pants are gone and when I go to lie back down on the bed he catches me and sets me on top of him again.

"You lead," Kovan tells me. "I will follow."

This time I freeze.

All my doubts come swirling back—*I can't be in charge, who am I to direct a sage*—

But then his hands, drifting up my sides, center me again.

And his eyes, steady, as Kovan says, "You can't break me, Tasa."

And I begin to understand that maybe I still don't understand what a sage is capable of.

Because he can see that deeply into me, and it's like he's somehow reached inside me and seen the darkest parts of me and bathed them in the light of his golden gaze.

"I don't think I'm ready yet," I whisper.

Kovan blinks, then nods. "Understood. Do you still want to... keep touching?"

Oh! "No, wait, yes, I mean—I don't want to stop."

But that he would have without any drama, not withdrawing and not demanding and just confirming what *I* want—that's heady.

Kovan's head tilts to the side. His hands resume stroking, and I shiver as he asks in a low voice, "What do you want, Tasa?"

Not need.

Want.

Though in this moment, they feel like the same thing.

He won't deny me. I know he won't.

It's the only thing that gives me the courage to ask another person for what I want:

"Can you touch me?" I whisper.

Taking one of his hands, I draw it down to the apex between my thighs. "Here."

Sitting as I am Kovan doesn't have a great view, but even when his finger barely touches me my breath hitches.

He glances up at my face. I don't know what he sees there, but his gaze goes focused.

And then Kovan starts methodically taking me apart.

It's like *he* is hyper-fixated on figuring out exactly what touch will bring me the most pleasure, and since him touching me at *all* like this is already a dream he does not have to work hard.

But he does.

Slowly, tentatively, then bolder and surer as he becomes more confident, cataloguing my every gasp and jerk until I am soaking and aching in an unreasonably quick time considering we've never had sex before and he's maybe *never* had sex—

And then he slides a finger into me while continuing to stroke and I stop breathing.

"Tasa?"

That low, sexy voice, still, always checking with me.

I shiver at the sound, and that moves his finger inside me, and abruptly I can't take it anymore.

I lift myself up off his hand and take hold of his hard length, running my thumb over the leaking precome as he hisses.

"I'm ready," I tell him.

No doubts. No fears.

"Then take what you want from me," Kovan tells me.

And wonder of wonders, I do.

I position him at my entrance and slowly slide down.

I'm plenty wet—I don't think I have *ever* been this wet, which under other circumstances I might be embarrassed about but not with him, and that's the difference—but still tight.

So I take him little by little, working onto his length as I pant.

Then Kovan touches my clit again and I clench around him for a second, and then my legs simply fall open wider.

"Good?" he asks me in a tight voice, circling my clit as I tremble.

"So good," I whisper.

Kovan bucks involuntarily at my words, and I only then really take notice of how still he's been holding himself for me. His jaw is clenched tight, his ab muscles stark with tension with the effort of making sure I have all the time I need to do what I want.

I take a breath and sink down further. "Move."

His gaze flicks up to mine, a dark question.

"*Move*, Kovan," I demand.

And this time, he does, thrusting up into me as I let out a strangled cry. My muscles clamp around him, but he keeps circling, keeps moving, and moments later he's seated fully within me.

I want to revel in that feeling, of being so full of him, all the power of him inside me and beneath me, but *I* am not the sage of resolve with perfect fucking discipline and now that we've started I can't stop.

I brace my hands on his shoulders, gasping for air as I rock over him. Kovan takes the opportunity to take one of my breasts in his mouth again as I mewl in pleasure.

His mouth on me, and his hands, and all of him with me and in me and my orgasm comes for me all at once, my muscles clenching him tight as I shake with the force of it.

I collapse kind of limply on his chest, trying to breathe through the aftershocks except then Kovan is kissing me again and stroking my back and who needs air anyway?

His cock twitches inside me as I stop rocking, though, and I realize he's still hard.

"You haven't come yet?" I whisper, astonished and maybe a little worried. Am I not enough for him after all? The man has been celibate for ages, honestly he should have gone off right away—

"Not until you've taken everything you want from me," Kovan says firmly.

Though he does involuntarily thrust into me again, just a little. My eyes widen. "Oh gods, is this your *resolve*? Are you serious?"

Kovan flashes a grin at me, and with him all sweaty beneath me that's enough to have me clenching around him again and he groans.

"You've taught me," Kovan manages to say, "to be creative. To—" His eyes lose focus when I deliberately clench my muscles around him.

Okay, maybe he is still human.

"To imagine more ways of being," Kovan gets out. "And I'm going to show you what I can do."

Oh my gods.

My voice is a whisper as I ask, a little shakily, "What are you going to do?"

"Bring you joy," he says simply. Easily. Like it's the most obvious thing in the world. "Bring you joy again and again and again. Whatever you want, Tasa."

I stare at him, overwhelmed.

This is what centered a sage, and his resolve.

Me.

Tears spill out of my eyes, and he frowns, starting to sit up—

"I love you," I breathe. "I already love you. You don't need—to—"

Kovan captures my mouth in a kiss, cutting off my words and opening fully to me.

He rolls us, with me beneath him now.

Only when we have to separate for air does Kovan say, "I *want* to, Tasa. I want *you*. I want to be yours and for you to be mine, to care for, to bring joy to, to *love*. Will you let me?"

Will I *let* him?

Will I ever be able to let him go, that's the real question.

No. The answer is no.

He wants to be mine? For me to be his? Then I am *keeping* him, and fuck the fucking priesthood.

"Will you take me like this?" I ask him. "Take me, claim me—"

Like no one else has ever wanted.

Like he is desperate to, which is so unbelievable and my heart is soaring with it because not only does someone want me, *this* incredible man, specifically, wants *me*, and when he begins to move again I can't help but moan.

But it's slow, so, so slow, and when I try to move faster Kovan catches my knees and spreads them wider, reaching even deeper inside me.

"Will you take me, Tasa?" Kovan asks, fucking me slowly, driving me higher and higher as I writhe beneath him. "Take me, just as I am, like this—"

"All of you, Kovan," I whisper, "all of me—"

"*Yes*—"

The angle shifts and I cry out as he strokes over a spot inside me no one has ever touched before, not like that, *just* like that—

Kovan does it again, and again, until I am practically sobbing beneath him from the pleasure of it, my orgasm building and holding me on the exquisite edge.

"Is this what you want, Tasa?" Kovan asks.

I manage to open my eyes, meet his golden, glowing gaze.

All his resolve, focused on bringing me joy.

Maybe that's not the sage, though.

That's just him.

Reaching up, I grip his hair tightly, locking us together.

"*You*, Kovan," I tell him fiercely. "I want *you*."

And that, finally, is what tips him over the edge.

The sage's perfect control shatters, and he drives into me.

I come in an instant, but still Kovan keeps going, the weight of him stroking into me through my aftershocks as I hold on, to him, to us, and then feeling him finally, finally let go inside of me.

Kovan shudders over me, and I reach up to push his hair away from his forehead and kiss him and kiss him and kiss him.

When we can finally breathe, he rolls off of me and I follow instinctively, tucking myself into his arms, which tighten around me just as instinctively.

"The tea," Kovan finally manages. "And your bed, I made a mess, I should—"

"Stay," I whisper. "You should stay."

I hear him swallow, and my heart clenches.

He doesn't know if he can stay.

He doesn't say things he doesn't mean.

But Kovan buries his face in the crook of my neck, breathing hard, and I think maybe I feel his tears as he says only, "Okay."

I will take it.

I will take him.

However I can get him, even if I don't deserve him.

That is *my* resolve.

CHAPTER 9

KOVAN

Tasa makes us tea.

I bake bread.

It's improved, but I can do better still.

Touch between us comes easily now, but always weighted.

I don't think I will ever take being able—being *allowed*—to touch her for granted.

It's almost as though our normal positions are reversed, in a way. With every touch from her, I lose track of what I was doing and focus entirely on her.

With every touch from me, she centers.

That, too, I cannot take for granted.

When we return to Crystal Hollow the next day, it's a whole new experience.

The village hasn't changed, but we have.

Or rather: we have become more at ease in ourselves.

I made a list of requests from Crystal Hollow for Tasa to choose from in case she wasn't feeling inspired—focus offered, but not trapping her into drudgery.

She built exactly one item from it in her workshop before having a better idea in the middle of the second and hyper-focusing on something entirely new and brilliant.

Now, in town, I defend her from people's demands to speed her way to her collection to finish the piece while she still feels the fire of invention.

I deliver the completed piece—imbued with dragon scale—to the woman who asked for it. When she goes to retrieve the payment in the coin that I insist on rather than dry goods, I take the opportunity to revisit everyone I can find about their requests and inform them of the new status quo.

Tasa stumbles when she returns from installing her new creation for Noten and hears me pitching her building abilities to Noten, whose sister-in-law's family needs more space for their growing family.

"Kovan! *My house is crooked*," she hisses at me, aghast.

"Crooked houses are actually more valuable, because they take greater skill, and they aren't boring," I continue to Noten in a normal tone. "Your niblings will be thrilled with a house so uniquely their own."

Noten snorts. "They probably will. Their parents will be glad of anything with walls that stand. Can you really do it, Tasa?"

"I mean—yes," she says, glancing at me wide-eyed. "Would you really trust me to?"

To Noten's credit, he doesn't glance at me for assurance.

He simply steps right up to Tasa, where everyone in eyesight can see.

"My stove has never worked so reliably," he says, raising his voice slightly. "Not a single blip. If you want to build another house, I'll be the first in line."

I manage not to shout my satisfaction, but it's a near thing.

Now Noten glances at me, and has the gall to wink.

I bite back a laugh and incline my head.

He's a better man than I gave him credit for.

Maybe they all are.

But the exhilaration is all at the sprouting from a seed that I planted.

Until I have restored the safety of Tasa's cottage, I will make it safe for her to be here, in Crystal Hollow. The first step is removing people's wariness of her—and I will help get dragon scales into every house that opens to her, to make them safe for her, to make that happen.

It's only one person whose behavior I've changed so far.

But changing even one person matters.

The weak infrastructure in Crystal Hollow isn't because of the shattered buildings; the shattered buildings merely reveal the weak infrastructure.

I could use my power as a sage to bring them all together for a moment, but that's not what Tasa needs. That won't *last*.

They need to support each other through all the moments.

That can't be built with a grand action from an outsider, but step by step, one act at a time.

Methodical, deliberate, difficult, thoughtful work—*that* is the domain of resolve.

"Hey!" It's the cantankerous old woman. "Priest man. Word is your friends are on their way across the water, and they don't look like folks coming to help. You going to do anything about that?"

It's also the work of a lifetime—

And time is the one thing I don't have.

"I'm not a priest," I tell her reflexively.

She snorts. "Sure you aren't. I wasn't born yesterday—"

"I'm a sage."

All around us, Crystal Hollow grows quiet.

Sages have that effect here, it seems.

I look at Tasa; see my own anxiety reflected back on me.

The seeds are planted, but they need time.

I will find a way to give it to them.

Even if I can't be here to see them bloom.

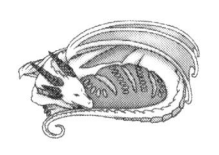

TASA

Kovan bows to my most irascible client. "I will head them off," he says. "Thank you for the warning."

The old woman nods. "There's truth to it, then? The rumors that the priests were trying to turn the sages against us for their own ends?"

She's making sure no one gets in Kovan's way, I realize.

Because of course there are people who would be relieved to see the priests. Some even crossed to the mainland to petition them, after the detonation, and have been holding out hope despite the weeks of priests demonstrably not rushing to our aid.

Kovan, though, doesn't know when someone is trying to help him—or is so scrupulously honest that he can't seize an opportunity when one smacks him in the face—because all he says is, "I do not know the specifics of what they wanted the Sage of Wrath to do. But I know what they have asked of me."

He takes a breath.

And looks at *me*.

"And I do not believe," the sage says quietly, but firmly, "that it is in Crystal Hollow's best interests for the Sage of Wrath's working to come down."

His words hang in the air.

Impossibly damning, coming from a sage.

With a mix of hopelessness—that we cannot expect help from that corner, even if most of us knew it—and hope—that maybe now we can create something new of our lives without their shadow.

"Well, what are you going to do about it?" the old woman asks.

His tortured gaze turns to me again, and I *know*.

I know what he is going to do, and my anxiety vanishes in a rush of anger.

"We're going to stop them, of course," I say briskly.

Kovan's gaze darkens. "This will be dangerous, Tasa. You should stay—"

"I deal with dangerous every day. I'm a null, remember?" I glare at him. "*Someone* told me recently that makes me powerful. Or is that only when you don't want an audience?"

Before he can respond, the old woman announces, "Good. Tasa's one of us. Someone from Crystal Hollow should be there. Get on now, both of you. Shoo!"

She whacks us both on the butt with a broom, which jolts me into action despite the way my brain is fritzing, and I take off at a run.

Of all people, *she* just claimed me for Crystal Hollow.

Accepted me as a *representative.*

Yes, okay, it's probably because this way she doesn't have to put herself in danger and also that if I get it wrong they'll feel comfortable disavowing whatever I decided—

But despite the fact that I moved to the mountain, and that I've caused her and everyone else countless problems over the years, I am still part of Crystal Hollow.

And I *do* get a say.

So when Kovan reaches for me as I hurry along, as if to stop me, to slow me down, I shake him off.

That is not what I need from him.

"Tasa," he growls.

"No," I snap. "You think I don't realize that you're planning on sacrificing yourself?"

He jerks back like I've struck him.

"You can take the scales past Yora's sphere of influence, and then they won't be able to connect anything to Zan," Kovan says urgently. "You won't be in trouble for harboring a dragon, or me—"

"Yes yes, you're very noble. They really did a good job with you, didn't they? You'll always jump to sacrifice yourself."

That finally gets through to him. He snaps, "I'm doing this for *you*."

"Well *I don't want it*." I whirl and shove him. "I want *you*, you absolute lunkhead!"

His eyes flash gold.

But then it fades, his expression growing pained.

It makes me madder.

"Is this your limit then?" I demand. "You try for one whole day, and that's all you have in you?"

"Tasa, I don't *have* more days—"

I start running again.

I am not waiting for anyone to see that I'm worth keeping.

Never again.

All that hiking up and down the mountain has been good for something, because I'm not even out of breath as I tell him, "*You* are the one who decides that. You could *try* to have more days, instead of showing me what we could have and then setting it on fire at the first sign of trouble. And don't you dare," I finish in a low voice, "ask me *how*."

He doesn't have an answer for that.

Of course he doesn't.

For someone I want so desperately, I'm doing a bang-up job of being a person no one will want to be around, just like always.

But this *is* me.

He wanted to respect my boundaries? That's true even when it isn't convenient.

And the contingent of priests on the narrow strip of land approaching the island is extremely not convenient.

Kovan puts on a burst of speed to beat me to the mouth of the island. I glare at him, but he can't see me—he's blocking their view of me.

Still trying to keep me safe.

But this is different than what he was doing in Crystal Hollow. There, he was trying to get them to see me differently, and yes it was like being in a bizarro world, but here he's trying to hide me.

No amount of hiding has ever made me safe.

I peek around him, not willing to step aside for a better view in case I'll be too far to yank Kovan back from doing something stupid.

He's only had days to undo a lifetime of learning. I wish I had more time to be patient with him about it, but if I need to bop him on the nose for a while until he gets his sacrificial urges out of his system, I'll do it.

If Kovan wants to choose me, I'll do a lot more than that.

Darkness claws inside of me.

He may *not* choose me—actual me, rather than what he thinks is best.

I'll be devastated forever, but I wouldn't blame him.

Learned Muka is at the front, and honestly she still looks terrible—they didn't give her much time to recover.

Or perhaps she didn't allow herself time, because she needed to prove her resolve to save her own skin.

The rest of the priests look a little strained, but nothing serious yet.

Damn, we should have let them step on the island to weaken them, I think as they and Kovan greet each other tensely. Too late now.

"The dragon—" Learned Muka starts.

"There is no dragon here for you," Kovan says.

Easily. Casually.

I do not say things I do not mean.

Ohhh shit.

The Learned eyes Kovan sadly. "Is that how it is, then?" she asks softly.

In unison, every priest behind her shifts into the same stance.

I don't know enough about magic to know what it means, other than the obvious, which is that they're about to fight.

And with all of them together, they might have enough magic to be a problem for a sage who can't do anything big here in the Quiet.

"Choose wisely, Sage Kovan," Learned Muka says. "Out of my great respect for you, I would prefer to avoid a fight. But I must have the dragon in exchange. If not the dragon, then I will return with you. You know one of you must be sacrificed."

I nearly fall over when Kovan replies, "Why?"

He's not giving up yet!

Learned Muka stares at him. "You *know* why—"

Aaand that's my cue.

Kovan isn't fighting alone. Not while I'm here.

I duck under Kovan's arm and plant myself in front of him. "Hi! I don't, though," I say brightly. "And on behalf of Crystal Hollow, I can absolutely confirm there is no dragon here. But even if there were, we do not do human sacrifices, so no! I'm afraid if that's all you're here for—not to help with the village that collapsed after your priests came to town? no?—then I'll have to ask you to leave."

Learned Muka barely glances at me. "It was not priests who created the Quieting. It was a sage." She looks back at Kovan. "A sage could undo it."

"Oh, but sages have tried, haven't they?" I continue with a big old smile. "We've seen several delegations come to the border and not come to check on us. Maybe this is the will of the gods, you know? Oh, yes, I know *you're* the experts on magic, but I assumed since no priests had been by to look, it was because it was outside of your field—"

"What are you *doing*," Learned Muka hisses at me. "Get out of the way—"

"No," I tell her calmly as my heart thumps. "Crystal Hollow is my home, and we do not sacrifice people. It's that simple. If that's a problem for you, then leave."

"I am trying to save your village, foolish girl," she snaps at me.

"I'm not any less valuable than anyone else, and neither is anyone else in Crystal Hollow."

Kovan has me trying to believe that.

"Not priests," I continue. "Not dragons." I look over my shoulder. "And not sages."

Kovan kept trying to gift me resolve, but I don't need resolve to know that.

What he gifted me was *himself*. And in seeing him—and seeing him, by himself, trying, and changing so much with so little—

Then I can try, too.

Even someone as ordinary and magic-less as me can do something.

If I try, and keep trying.

If I take a stand, like I challenged him to.

Now it's my turn.

I look at Learned Muka's apoplectic expression—leaning into my skills here—and reach out to her.

She jerks back, but inexorably, I place my hand on her shoulder.

I don't feel anything happen when I nullify someone's magic. I never do.

But Learned Muka's face drains of color as she looks at me in horror.

"If you want the sage, you'll have to go through me," I tell her. "And I don't think you want to go through me."

KOVAN

I'M REELING IN AWE of Tasa.

At the clarity of her judgment.

At the boldness of her vision.

At the strength of her resolve.

But the priests don't see what I do—they only see a woman who has dared touch a Learned, and they react, beginning as one to move through an attack form.

I want to jump in front of Tasa, to shield her—

But I already decided she didn't need a shield, didn't I?

What she *needs* from me is to change people's hearts.

So I fall into my own form, and begin to move, too.

Tasa continues to speak—to use her prodigious skill at turning a confrontation, at managing people, at making them like her and see her as a person—and nothing I can do is more powerful than her words.

They've moved me, after all.

So what can a sage do?

What can *I* do?

I can have her back, always.

I think as I move, and since the priests don't know what I'm doing—Muka will recognize this from me as a kind of meditation as I gather my power, but she's not the one preparing to attack—they abort their attack form, shifting seamlessly to a defensive one.

A form designed to repel overwhelming offensive force.

Thinking, thinking.

With the dragon scales in my pocket, I could *change* the priests' minds. But like in Crystal Hollow, it wouldn't last. As soon as they return to the priesthood with their reports, they'll be back with even more priests.

Not least because, having seen one dragon scale, they might realize what I've managed, and that will doom more than just Zan.

But every seed planted has a chance to bloom.

Every heart that changes is one more.

Abruptly, I shift my movements, at once sure of what is needed from me—

What *I* need from myself.

This is the Sage of Wrath's legacy, and what I can be proud as the Sage of Resolve to take further than she could:

Planting my feet in the ground behind Tasa and saying *no more*.

And not just taking a stand, but *continuing* to try, because it's Yora who created the wall the priests will break against.

It's for me to turn the tide back against them.

I—*we*—are outnumbered.

Realizing I wasn't ready to attack, the priests have shifted back to an offensive form while they can.

I can't use overwhelming magic to defeat them without bringing worse down on us.

But I can find new ways to use my power beyond the narrow way the priesthood locked me into.

The priests, moving together, manifest a sphere of white magic.

The same magic that damaged even a dragon's wings; a threat.

One I do not heed.

The golden glow of my magic appears around me, so the priests will know that I am doing something, but not what.

Learned Muka frowns mightily as she tries to work it out—she, of the priests here, is the only one who knows enough of sage training to do so.

But she has never seen me do this.

I invert the forms.

Make my movements smaller, subtler; softer.

Quietly, quietly.

The golden aura around me expands to fill the space between me and the priests, breaking against Tasa like a river meeting a rock and moving around her.

THE QUIET SIDE

The priests launch their magic sphere at me—

But my gold working reaches them.

And the sphere of their magic dissipates as it moves toward us until it disperses harmlessly.

The priests rush back to their familiar forms by force of training, looking baffled—and afraid, and desperate, and angry—

But not resolved.

And the strength of the priesthood is in their unity of purpose. Break that, and victory is inevitable.

That's *why* I, as the Sage of Resolve, have so often been called to battlefields: to strengthen that unity.

I have, in fact, spent my whole life learning how to do that.

So I also know how to break it.

Learned Muka swears as she realizes what I've done.

But she doesn't make any move to stop me; as though, even knowing I am undoing the priests' resolve and thus their focus, and in so doing rendering them powerless, my mentor can't decide if she should.

Tasa doesn't miss a beat, continuing to make her case—for why we should all get to live, and freely. How the Quieting prevented a greater wrong, and created an opportunity, and *space*, for the priests to reconsider.

I don't miss a beat either, continuing to move.

Letting someone else lead, yes.

But it's Tasa, who I have *chosen* to trust.

And how I support her is up to *me*.

Little by little, using my power to widen the cracks inside them that she can pour into.

Planting a seed. Giving it time to grow.

A small magic that can become big, with the sheer volume of more hands working at the problem.

Tasa keeps trying.

I keep working.

And together, we turn back the tide.

Until the priests aren't even trying, but looking to Learned Muka for direction, or help, or, perhaps, forgiveness.

Learned Muka looks at me like she's never seen me before.

And perhaps she hasn't.

"Priests, retreat," she says. "I believe the Sage of Resolve and I can have words civilly."

"And the representative from Crystal Hollow," Tasa and I both add in unison.

Tasa flashes me a grin, a little wild.

I feel it too, thrumming inside me.

When the priests have retreated out of earshot, I don't wait for Learned Muka to control the dialogue, but instead tell her, "Every priest you send after me, or the dragon, or the barrier, I will undermine. Every act against me I will use to foment rebellion in the priesthood. It takes barely any power at all, Learned—merely dedication. I invite you to report that to the priesthood, if they would challenge the Sage of Resolve."

After a moment of studying me, she says neutrally, "That will be a lot of work."

I smile and meet Tasa's gaze. "The work of a lifetime," I agree.

This is how I will matter.

It will be arduous, painstaking, patient work. The priesthood is entrenched, and I may not see results of the work for years or more.

But that's why it's a task for resolve.

And with Tasa at my side, the hill we have to climb looks a lot less steep.

Then Tasa suggests, "You could also *not* report that to them."

Learned Muka looks at her, really looks.

And she *smiles*.

"An excellent thought," Learned Muka says. "It will take them a while to realize what you're doing, and in that time you can do a lot of damage."

I blink, startled that a woman of *her* resolve can change course so easily.

Then again: I did.

And she has always tried to support me, as best she knew.

"What will you do, then?" Tasa asks.

"You work from the outside," Learned Muka says, "and I will work from within."

She salutes Tasa, who startles and nods awkwardly in acknowledgement.

And then Learned Muka, who has been with me my whole life, turns to me.

She bows low—not as to a sage, but as to an emperor.

My breath catches in my throat.

But then I do what Tasa would not, out of an overabundance of caution.

And I step forward to hug her.

Learned Muka freezes in my embrace.

And then she lets out a breath, and a lifetime of preconceived notions with it as she relaxes.

When she withdraws, she orders Tasa, "Take care of him. He's special."

"I know," Tasa says, her voice choked.

Then Learned Muka smirks at me and takes her own leave.

"What was that face for?" Tasa asks.

I smile; a real smile, even as I watch the woman who helped make me who I am walk away into danger. "She knows that she doesn't need to tell me that you're special, too."

Tasa looks at me wide-eyed.

"So. We uh. Did we actually do that?" She gestures limply at the stretch of land already being lost to the tides, her hand beginning to shake as the heroic needs of the moment wash away with them.

I gather her in my arms.

"We did," I confirm.

And then I kiss her.

And with it, this time, at last, I promise her forever.

EPILOGUE

KOVAN

I AM WRITING A new entry in the book when large magic incoming pings my senses. I hurry outside and am just in time as Zan, still in his enormous dragon form, lands in the wildflower-covered space between Tasa's cottage—*our* cottage, now—and Celestial Sanctuary Temple.

For a moment, we just watch each other.

It's been months since we faced off against each other. Since Zan rescued me, and abandoned me to find my fate.

Reminded of my failure of manners that happened next when I first met Tasa, I clear my throat. "I'm glad your scales appear to have healed. If you're looking for Tasa, she should be back shortly—"

"You're still here."

It's not a question, but I answer anyway. "I am."

Zan studies me.

I resist the urge to fall into a form.

If he'd wanted me dead, he could have simply dropped me.

Then again, maybe he's changed his mind—

"I expected that the priests would try to find me," Zan says slowly.

I nod. "I've been working on that. The priesthood *is* still sending people—Crystal Hollow is alerting me." A community effort spearheaded by none other than the cantankerous old woman, who now demands I call her by her name, Nima, without any honorifics ("performative frills," she scoffed). "But I believe they may finally be beginning to notice that every priest they send after either of us returns substantially less zealous than they started."

The dragon *blinks*.

I smile. Maybe *I* have finally startled *him*.

So I take a breath and tell him, "No one besides Tasa is aware, but I have also been making use of the scales you left behind to address the magical void left in Yora's wake. If you don't object, I would like to continue that effort, to strengthen the village against outside threats by removing their dependence on the priesthood."

Another blink. "Why?"

Here it goes. I take a breath.

I've known I would need to convince him for months.

"Because Yora started something powerful here, but she didn't finish it. I think we can build something here that matters." I meet Zan's gaze directly. "A sanctuary in truth for anyone who needs it, be they dragon or sage."

His pupils contract. It's the only reaction he makes, but in his otherwise preternatural stillness it's enough.

Then Tasa bursts onto the scene. "Zan, you're awake!" She hurtles toward him, and Zan startles back a step.

Ha. Even *I* couldn't make him back up as easily as Tasa does without trying.

She has always been a force.

Now, she believes it.

"Oh, I'm so sorry," Tasa says quickly. "Kovan says my null powers don't affect your scales, but I guess that's not the same as you—and anyway I should have asked first if you even like being hugged—"

"*Hugged?*" Zan echoes incredulously.

My shoulders shake with silent laughter.

Seeing this seems to make Zan even more aghast, because clearly I know that Tasa meant it.

She scowls at me. "Look, I'm *sorry*, but I went to visit Noten and then he was at the house I built and the new baby's arrived! And I maybe got a little into the snuggling mode—"

My laughter finally breaks free, clear and delighted.

My plan to rehabilitate Crystal Hollow has been working, slowly but surely. Tasa spends more and more time there without rushing home.

Because she's able to touch people—figuratively *and* literally.

"*Anyway*." Tasa huffs. "Zan, can we get you something to eat? We have fresh-baked bread."

A thing she can assume now; that she has come to be able to rely on.

"I thought you couldn't bake bread," Zan says, sounding more baffled by the moment.

Tasa points at me. "*He* does. You've never had bread this good, I promise."

Zan looks at me again.

Probably the dragon didn't expect much from me when he left me here.

After a long moment, his magic shimmers, and in place of a dragon is the same ethereally beautiful man who gave me the push to change my life.

"I didn't expect you to stay," Zan tells me.

To defend him, he means. "I know. But you should have been able to. So know now that I'm not going anywhere."

"And after you've made this a sanctuary?" he challenges.

I don't blink. "Then I will still be here, doing the work to make sure it is in truth."

Tasa comes up beside me and takes my arm. Zan's gaze drops down to where we're connected, but I can't read his expression.

"I can teach trades to anyone who comes here to start over!" Tasa says excitedly. "I've learned enough of them, after all. And Kovan is working on a book especially for sages." She squeezes my arm. "For when we've passed. And whoever follows us can keep adding to it."

Beginning with instructions for how to bake bread.

But not ending there.

"Come on, we'll show you," Tasa prompts. "And feed you. And then ask you again about your scales, but I promise we'll continue supplying you with the best bread even if you say no—"

"My love, if you're trying to convince him we're *not* trying to extort him, this is not the way," I interrupt with amusement.

Zan snorts agreement.

Tasa stomps her foot in irritation. "How are you so much better at talking to people when I'm the one who's had to do it my whole life?"

I give her a quick kiss on the cheek. "Your words count when it matters, love."

She smiles up at me, blushing just a little, and as ever, it makes me want to hold onto her and never let her go.

But I'm just in time to see something in Zan's gaze as he watches our easy affection—perhaps the casualness of it?—before it's gone.

"If you need a moment..." he says, glancing away—

Toward the temple.

Toward Yora.

"Oh! Thank you," Tasa says brightly. "You can go on in ahead of us, we'll be right there. Help yourself to anything."

Zan freezes again.

And Tasa proves me right by speaking again before he can, "Of course you're welcome in our home, Zan."

Zan stares at her.

Then he looks at me and says, "There are more scales in the grass."

As if I hadn't noticed them.

But this is, if not explicit permission, then at least an opening.

A start.

One I can build on.

Zan turns toward the door, where the pot that used to be inside of our bedroom has begun to sprout, past the planters Tasa made for me with materials she'd carried up the mountain the day we met.

My work there isn't done yet.

Gardening, I've found, is an even more appropriate scope for a sage of resolve than bread-baking.

As Zan almost reverently enters the home Tasa built for us, she turns to me with a wide smile.

Taking a moment just for us, to connect; to *be*—who we are, to ourselves and to each other, and not what other people see.

I hold out my arms, and Tasa steps into them confidently, joyfully, as if it's the most natural thing in the world for two such different people to embrace each other in all that we are.

When she kisses me, the world doesn't fade; my heart soars, and my mind is crystal-clear:

This is where I am meant to be.

This is the world I will spend every day creating for us.

I hear the sweet sound of birdsong all around us, the sun warming my face, the mountain air crisp and fresh.

Every day, no matter what comes, I will make the days this beautiful for her.

And for us.

That is my resolve.

In 500 years, the *Sage of Wrath* wakes up.
And a certain dragon has been waiting for her.

Preorder Book 1 of the Sage's Sanctuary trilogy, The Quiet Light, *and sign up for bonus scenes with characters from* The Quiet Side *at caseyblair.com*!

THANK YOU

Thank you for reading!

The Quiet Side is a prequel to my upcoming cozy fantasy romance trilogy in the Sage's Sanctuary world, beginning with *The Quiet Light*. As I was beginning to tease out the threads that make up that story, I kept circling back to how this isolated mountain cottage came to be—and how resistance can be born from the smallest acts, and how they grow, and change beyond what we imagine for them. When an image came into my mind of an enthusiastic woman hammering a roof where a too-serious powerful magic user was in hiding, I knew I had to start with their story, and *The Quiet Side* is what came out.

If you enjoyed reading *The Quiet Side*, I hope you'll tell someone about it or leave a review!

For a FREE, newsletter-exclusive short stories featuring characters from *The Quiet Side*, sign up for my newsletter at caseyblair.com! Subscribing will keep you in the loop on free fiction opportunities, sales, and new books—including when *The Quiet Light*, the first book in Yora and Zan's series, goes live.

I will also be serializing *The Quiet Light* on Patreon as I write it, so take a look if you want to be the first to read the story!

Happy reading!
Casey

About the Author

Casey Blair is a bestselling author of hopeful fantasy novels about ambitious women who dare, including the Sage's Sanctuary, Diamond Universe, and Tea Princess Chronicles series. Her own adventures have included teaching English in rural Japan, taking a train to Tibet, rappelling down waterfalls in Costa Rica, and practicing capoeira. She now lives in the Pacific Northwest and can be found dancing spontaneously, exploring forests around the world, or trapped under a cat.

For more information visit her website caseyblair.com or follow her on Instagram @CaseyLBlair.

ALSO BY

Sage's Sanctuary
The Quiet Side (prequel)
The Quiet Light

Diamond Universe: Sierra Walker
Take Back Magic
Take Back Demons
Take Back Worlds

Sundered Realms
The Sundered Realms

Tea Princess Chronicles
A Coup of Tea
Tea Set and Match
Royal Tea Service

Stand-Alone
When Legends Spark
The Sorceress Transcendent
Consider the Dust

Made in the USA
Columbia, SC
03 June 2025